Of The Side Of Jesus Ignatius

The Christian armed against the seductions of the world and the illusions of his own heart

Of The Side Of Jesus Ignatius

The Christian armed against the seductions of the world and the illusions of his own heart

ISBN/EAN: 9783741189999

Manufactured in Europe, USA, Canada, Australia, Japa

Cover: Foto ©Andreas Hilbeck / pixelio.de

Manufactured and distributed by brebook publishing software (www.brebook.com)

Of The Side Of Jesus Ignatius

The Christian armed against the seductions of the world and the illusions of his own heart

ADVERTISEMENT.

THE greater part of this little book was found translated in manuscript among the papers of the late Father Ignatius Spencer. The book is so valued in Italy, that it was thought well to publish it in these countries. The author, Father Ignatius, of the Side of Jesus, died in SS. John and Paul's Retreat, Rome, May 26, 1844, in the 43rd year of his age. He has left several other works, *The Life of Ven. Vincent M. Strambi*, a *Treatise on Sacred Eloquence*, and some other manuals of piety, one of which, *The School of Jesus Crucified*, will be shortly published in English.

PREFACE.

To the Christian Reader.

There is nothing more beneficial and important than the attentive reading and reflecting over a good book—I mean a book of piety. We find here the most faithful friend, the most secure guide, the most sincere counsellor; one who never flatters us, but consoles, enlightens, and encourages us; and if he reproves, contradicts, humbles, or threatens us, we listen to him, without being put out with him, without being put to shame, without being much disturbed. A quarter of an hour's entertainment with a pious book elevates, moves, carries away the soul, and raises it even to God ; it penetrates the mind till it reaches the heart, and puts its affections in order, and corrects its wanderings. The heart it is which leads us astray ; the heart is the source of those numberless illusions which entice us to our destruction : now, a good book has the heart particularly in view, and hence it produces those wonderful changes which we are so often astonished at.

This is what has determined me to make a selection of dogmatic and moral speculation, and practical truths, which are met with scattered here and there in the works of ascetic authors, and of the many virtuous writers who treated of them (to whom, therefore, is due, almost entirely, whatever value may be attached

to this my work), and to present them to
the Christian reader in this little book,
in order to procure for him those infinite
benefits which result from devout reading.
That infernal spirit which stirs in the
misbelievers of our times, never for a
moment relaxes its efforts to promote vice
and spread impiety, by means of insidious
productions under a thousand forms of
error and seduction. It, therefore, will
not be superfluous to increase the number
of good books, and present them to the
public under various aspects, in order to
meet the tastes and the wants of all and
each, and by this means to spread good
principles, to extend the empire of virtue,
and thus, in some degree, to make head
against the masters of error. On this
account, I have thought well to entitle
this little book "THE CHRISTIAN ARMED,"

because the evangelical truths treated in it are calculated to defend the Christian against the attacks of the enemies of his salvation, and to guard him in an especial manner against the seductions of the world.

I have wished to treat and to draw out the truths proposed by means of very short reflections, because in this way they are the better impressed on the memory, and are less tedious to the reader, who finds at a glance the truth he is seeking.

One single truth of the Gospel, read composedly, meditated on attentively in its principle, in its end, in its object, taking in view its efficacy, its omnipotent virtue, is more precious than any other book, and produces more fruit than anything else that can be read ; but to gather

this fruit, you must read with simplicity ;
in order to be nourished by the language
of faith, you must read little and meditate
much—read with the heart rather than
with the spirit, and with the mind more
than with the eye.   Let the truths which
you read penetrate you, digest what you
have read, and convert it, by means of
suitable resolutions, into your own proper
substance ; make a pause from time to
time, interrupting your reading with holy
aspirations, and it will become a real conversation with God ; endeavour to love
exceedingly each truth, to impregnate
your soul with it, to find your rest in it,
to delight in it, to assimilate your inmost
feelings with it. ·In this way, reading
little, and meditating much, you will become, by the light of faith, learned in the
science of the saints, and God will teach

you all things : you will begin to hate vanity, and to love truth ; being made strong and valorous in faith, you will fight against sin, against your passions, against the seductions of the world, and, by the grace of God, you will gain the victory.

And in order, in a single little book, you may find easily whatever will interest your piety, I have endeavoured to bring together, in the Second Part, all those practices of devotion and prayers which may serve as nourishment to your spirit in approaching the sacraments, assisting at Mass, or on other occasions, not omitting to propose some short considerations on the Passion of Jesus Christ: The sweetest recompense of this my labour, such as it is, will be : If I succeed in bringing back any soul from the way of perdition, if I can inspire all with a sincere love of religion and piety, and co-operate towards the eternal salvation of the souls redeemed by the blood of Jesus Christ. May our Lord be pleased to realize this my desire!

THE CHRISTIAN ARMED,

&c. &c.

PART I.

INSTRUCTION FOR MEDITATION.

1. Before you begin to read and meditate on some truth, recollect yourself for a moment, and place yourself, with lively faith, in the presence of God; adore him with all humility, offer him, with the utmost affection, all you are, and pray to him for light in your understanding to know this truth, and strength in your will to embrace it. Put before yourself the particular fruit which you desire to reap from the Meditation; for example, to escape from some particular sin, to practice some virtue, earnestly begging it from God.

2. This done, read with attention the points of the Meditation, weighing well the words, and pausing at anything which causes a stronger impression. Reflect on what you have to believe and to do in regard to the truth you have before you; what you are moved to by it as useful, as necessary, or as just; what evil may follow in case you neglect it. Ask yourself: *What instruction do I find in the truth or mystery before me, for the correction of my life? Have I lived in conformity with the truths and maxims on which I am meditating?* Strive to convince your understanding of it, and to impress it deeply upon it. Examine then what account you make of a truth so important for your salvation: whether you are accustomed to regulate your life according to its teaching, or whether you neglect it, observing and noting in what; and what evil consequences have followed. Accuse yourself before God of your negligence and your faults; examine the reason of them, and forecast what you

will have to do or to avoid for the time
to come.

3. In the third place, go on to the
affections of the will, which will vary
according to the variety of the matter.
The following will be found frequently
suitable: Affections of confusion and
of sorrow, of diffidence in yourself, of
confidence in the goodness of God and
in the merits of Jesus Christ, of thanksgiving, of oblation of yourself, of
resignation, &c. Then make firm resolutions, and form serious intentions
of practising for the future what in
the Meditation you have learned and
known it is your duty to do. It is
necessary, however, to go into detail.
For example: I will practise this or
that virtue, ... on this or
that occasion, . . . by the use of
such and such means. . . . I will
fly from this or that vice. . . . Stir
yourself to enter on a life entirely
different from that which you led
till now, and wholly opposed to the
lying maxims of the world, to the
allurements of sense, and to the sug-

gestions of the devil, and conformable in everything to the Gospel of Jesus Christ.

4. Conclude with an affectionate colloquy with our Lord, begging him for grace to put into execution what you have resolved. Give him thanks for the lights which he has imparted to you, and offer yourself without reserve to his divine service, and to his holy love. Turn, also, to our blessed Lady, imploring her assistance to keep yourself faithful to God.

PREPARATORY PRAYER BEFORE MEDITATION.

O my God, my Creator, my last end, and my all, I firmly believe that thou art here present; that I am wholly in in thee, and thou wholly in me; that thy divine eyes are on me, as if I were the one only being about whom thy thoughts are occupied. In this conviction, with which faith inspires me, I adore thee, O my God, with the most profound reverence of which a miserable creature like me is capable. I unite my most wretched adorations with those which thou receivest from the angels and saints in heaven, and from just souls on earth.

I offer thee this meditation, O my God. I intend to make it for thy glory, and for the salvation of my soul. I renounce all the distractions which I might have, through the levity of my own spirit, and through the artifices of the enemy of my salvation.

O adorable Trinity, Father, Son, and Holy Ghost, to thee I consecrate my memory, my understanding, and my will. Give me the necessary attention, and the lights and affections which thou seest to be the most suitable for drawing benefit from this meditation.

From thee, O lovely Saviour of my soul, I expect this assistance and those graces. Dispose my spirit and my heart to comprehend what thou desirest of me, and to execute it with fidelity. Teach me what I ought to ask; show me the right way to ask it. Without thee all my efforts are in vain.

Most holy Mary, mother of my God, and my mother, my angel guardian, you my holy advocates, obtain for me the grace to begin this holy meditation well, and to conclude it with the fruit which God expects from me. Amen.

ACT OF THANKSGIVING AND PRAYER AFTER MEDITATION.

O my God, my most generous Benefactor, my most loving Father, I thank thee, with feelings of the most lively gratitude, for all the lights and good inspirations which thou hast in thy goodness imparted to me in the time of my meditation. I beseech thee, perfect by thy grace the work of thy mercy; and seeing that thou hast made me to know and to desire what is good, assist me to perform it. Imprint deeply on my spirit and on my heart the truths on which I have been meditating, and give me grace to take them always as the safe rule of my life; so that, conforming all my actions to the maxims of the Gospel, it may be my happy lot to share in those eternal goods which that same Gospel promises to those who have faith, quickened by charity.

MAXIM I.

"What doth it profit a man to gain the whole world, if he lose his soul?"

Reflections.

1. The matter here in question is not losing or winning a lawsuit; it is

not being happy or unhappy through the whole course of your life. This would be an important matter, but it would not be of infinite importance. It would be important, but a failure would not be without remedy. What concerns us here is happiness or unhappiness eternal; whether you will possess God eternally with the blessed, or be cast headlong into the eternal flames of hell. This is what we speak of when we speak of saving the soul. Death comes, and in the moment of death all is lost, all flies away; this great world shall entirely vanish. What will become of me, if I lose my soul? If from my bed I pass into eternal fire, who will comfort me for my lot, who will repair my loss—what will it then avail me to have been rich, great, and honoured—what will the whole world avail me, if I had possessed the whole world? Nothing. If the soul is lost, all is lost. Shall I not think of this?

2. Those great men, who have made a name, what are they the better

now for having made such a noise in the world, having made such great gains, having enjoyed every pleasure, if now they are damned? What does it avail them that they have shone in the world, that they have gained great renown, that they have satisfied every passion, if they are burning, raging, and despairing in hell? They have then lost all, and the whole world has profited them nothing. They have led a hard life, full of agitation and disquietude—they have sacrificed their rest, their health, their very life, for the sake of enjoying the world, its delights, its pleasures, its riches. But, then, they have lost their soul; they have lost all, irremediably and for ever. And shall I choose to put myself in the way to meet so lamentable a fate?

3. I exist in the world, not to become rich, not to enjoy the world, but to save my soul. This is the one thing necessary. This is the great, the principal, the only affair. If, when you leave the world, you gain

salvation, and put your soul in safety, though you may not have succeeded in anything else, you have gained eternal happiness; but if, in quitting the world, after having gone through great toils and great struggles—after having made great gains, you lose your soul, then you have done nothing. You have neglected the greatest of all affairs, you have ruined that which, properly speaking, was your only affair, that for which you were in the world, and you have ruined it for ever. Do you believe this truth, and do you think with such indifference on the affair of your eternal salvation, and do you spend the whole of your life through about any or everything, besides gaining salvation for your soul? Nay, do you expose, at every moment, your soul to the risk of being lost? Is this impiety or is it madness?

Fruit.—Renew, every morning, when you say your morning prayer, the firm resolution to employ yourself in earnest about the affair of your salvation. Say to yourself, many times in the day, while you are busy about your office, when you are commencing an act, when you go to your work, when you are tempted, *What does it avail me to gain all the world, if I lose my soul? What will be the good of gain, of pleasure, of gratification, of pastimes, of toils, if I do not save my soul?* This practice is most useful, and suitable to every sort of person. This truth, duly penetrated, is enough to make you reform your whole life. Does your conscience reproach you that you have done nothing for your eternal salvation? Begin to-day, because this day may be the last portion of time which the Lord gives you to work out the salvation of your soul.

MAXIM II.

To gain salvation for our soul, we must do ourselves continual violence.

Reflections.

1. The affair of salvation is a difficult and thorny affair. The kingdom

of heaven, says Jesus Christ, can be gained only by force, and those only can carry it away who do themselves violence. The difficulties in the way of salvation are real difficulties. On all sides we meet with obstacles which would keep us from it; and if we do not do ourselves continual violence to overcome them, it will not be gained. Everywhere we meet with enemies laying snares for our destruction. If we do not use continual efforts to conquer them, we shall become their victims. The road which leads to heaven is a strait road; it is a narrow road, overlayed with thorns, and full of dangers. No man will walk on it long but he who, doing violence to himself, embraces humility, penance, and mortification. People know this, they acknowledge it, and yet they live as if the affair of salvation was the easiest of all affairs. They agree that there is no other way to lead the soul to salvation but the way taught by Jesus Christ, and yet they walk by the broad way of the world, of the multitude, of fashion; there is no watch kept, no attention paid to the mortification of the passions, no effort made to oppose the enemies of salvation; and yet people trust they will be saved. At what price do you expect the kingdom of heaven, if you refuse the most trifling price of doing yourself a little violence?

2. The affair of salvation is a most delicate affair; it requires care, vigilance, attention in the highest degree. This life is all temptation. Our most dangerous tempters are ourselves; our own heart betrays us, and the heaviest storms have their birth on our own ground. Bad examples draw back from what is good; the corruption, the seductions of the world impel us to evil. What has to be inferred from all this? Is it not that we must continually have our arms in hand, and that we must do ourselves continual violence to repel the furious assaults of our passions, which seek to ruin us, and to escape being carried away with the stream of wickedness, and of the

wicked, to the eternal loss of the soul? And yet, good God! people live delicately in the licentiousness of fashion; they refuse nothing to their own desires, to their own senses. Mortification, doing violence to their own inclinations, efforts to preserve innocence; these are ideas unknown to a great part of Christians. For some earthly affair, for any matter which interests them, what will they not do, what fatigues they undergo, what sacrifices they make, what exertions they use! while, to save the soul, nothing is done, no labour is undertaken, and the least violence discourages and terrifies. And do people expect, then, to gain salvation by an idle life, by a life of pleasure, by a useless life? Ah! my Lord, whatever violence it costs me, I will be saved.

3. Consider the way of life followed by all the saints. There is no saint who has not done himself continual violence; not one who has not, with unceasing efforts, combated his own passions. The saints, of every age, of

either sex, of every condition, have passed their lives in the painful exercises of the most austere penance. So many millions of martyrs have thought it not too much to give their blood in most horrible torments to save their souls. What purity of manners have not the saints observed! what horror have they not had for sin! what delicacy of conscience, always in war against their own inclination; always on their guard against the seductions of the world; always engaged in the great business of their salvation! Why was all this? which, however much, was not too much, because they chose to save their souls: and what can I hope for being so unlike to them? Was it that the saints were of another religion than mine? Had they another Gospel different from mine? Did they look for another reward different from that which I look for? No; then, what senseless folly is mine, to be so afraid of doing too much to make sure of eternal salvation, to have such a horror of the very name of penance, of mortification, of doing violence to my passions. Shall I reach the point that the saints have reached, if I walk by a road the very opposite to theirs?

Fruit.—Examine your life; and seeing it so unlike the life of the saints, say to yourself, Do I intend to be saved? Do I intend to gain possession of heaven? The way which leads to it is very narrow. Then I must do violence to my bad inclinations, especially to that *N.* (name it). I must resist my passions, especially that *N.* (name it), which is my predominant one. I must embrace abstinence, mortification, penance. I must not allow myself to be overcome by bad example, but must follow the example of the saints. Out of all this make an efficacious resolution, and offer it to the Lord, praying him to give you grace to keep it until death.

MAXIM III.

We must incessantly labour in order to gain our salvation.

Reflections.

1. To labour for our own salvation is to hate sin, seriously to quit it. It is to withdraw effectually from the occasions of sin; to work indefatigably at subduing our passions, at repressing the irregular desires of our heart. To labour for our own salvation is to follow constantly the maxims of Jesus Christ; to fashion our own life according to the principles of the Gospel; to make war with the world, which is the enemy of Jesus Christ. To labour for our own salvation is to root out from our own heart the love of creatures, in order that the love of God may reign there alone; it is to consider the affair of our own salvation as our great affair, which deserves and commands our undivided attention. Now speak with sincerity: Is there any time of life in which we are dispensed

from doing all this ? Is there any day of our life which has not been given to us by God to gain salvation; and you, how much time have you employed in this great affair? On what day of your life have you applied yourself in earnest to the salvation of your soul? All the saints have never given themselves rest. but have continually laboured to gain heaven. Do you suppose that, now-a-days, Paradise is given at a less price?. Did it then cost so dear to our saints, and would it be given to us for nothing? Ah! we must rather say our negligence in labouring for salvation is too clear a mark of our damnation.

2. God has not thought that doing what he has done was purchasing our salvation at too great a price, and shall we think it is doing too much to labour continually to reach salvation? What concern was it to God that we should be saved; and yet could he have done more than he did for our salvation? He made himself man to save men; he led a life of thirty-three years in poverty,

in labours, in sufferings, and finished it with the most cruel of all deaths. Is it a matter interesting to us to be saved? What a question to ask! Why then do we take so little pains about it? Why consume the best years of our life in vanity, in pastimes, in pleasures? Why put off labouring for our salvation to an old age, which is always uncertain? If we managed the least of our affairs in such a way as this, we should unquestionably despair of ever succeeding; and the most important affair of salvation, which calls for the diligent exertions of the entire life, and for which the Redeemer of men has laboured so much—is this what you treat with such indifference? O my God, what will become of me, if I do not begin from this day to labour in earnest for the salvation of my soul?

3. It would certainly be reasonable that we should concern ourselves about our salvation, and should labour for it with as much earnestness as the devil labours for our destruction.

Making this comparison is disgraceful for a Christian, and, nevertheless, the devil does make more account of our soul, and is more in earnest and diligent to ruin it than we are to save it.   What does he not do to put a soul in the way of perdition! What assiduity in tempting! What vigilance to avail himself of every occasion to do it! But however long the resistance may be, he is never weary with the conflict; he never relaxes in his endeavours; never gives up his assaults; he has recourse to every artifice for the ruin of a soul. Ah! my God, is it from the devil we must learn the esteem which we must have for our soul?   Is it possible that we must learn the way to labour continually for our salvation from the continual diligence which he uses to send us to perdition? Will not all this be sufficient to constrain you to labour seriously every day, every moment, to gain your salvation? Who gives you security but that the moment in which you lay aside your diligence and your earnestness about your salvation, may not be that very important moment on which it depends?

Fruit.—All the time of your life God gives you to employ in the great affair of your salvation. Do not then lose even one moment, but labour without ceasing to save your soul. Make the resolution every morning to employ the whole of that day in this all-important affair. Determine particularly what you will do all that day to merit Paradise; that you will, for instance, part from such and such company; that you will remedy, by a speedy confession, the disorders of your soul, visit the church, mortify your senses, &c. Some practical resolution of this kind.

MAXIM IV.

No man is wise, but the man who labours without ceasing in the business of his salvation.

Reflections.

1. Wisdom consists in taking suit-

able means to reach our end. A mistake in the choice of means for our salvation is perdition; and does the man deserve to be called wise who loses his soul? To possess the brightest genius, the greatest conceivable acuteness, and not to know how to distinguish false goods from real; how to avoid the seductive and deceitful snares of the enemies of our salvation; to throw ourselves after the shadows of vanity, after the phantasms of beauty; to destroy one's health, and life itself, to gain a post, which is no sooner gained than lost; to obtain a title, which vanishes in a moment; never to have a thought to eternity; to reach the end of life without ever having spent one day in the work of salvation; to be lost, and to have taken all possible means to be lost: should a man like this be called wise, and not rather a fool? And yet the world is full of such fools. Have you acted in any other way till now; have you ever thought that you had been created for God, and to possess God; have you taken the means necessary for arriving at this great end? And when do you, then, expect to become wise?

2. He is not a wise man who neglects and lets his own affairs go to ruin to attend to those of others. The affair of salvation is our own personal affair; all other affairs are foreign to us. To take pains that the affairs of one's house, of one's family, of one's city, of the state, should go on well; to work continually to increase one's property, about speculation and gains in trade, and to neglect the affair of salvation; to pay no attention, to take no pains to save the soul: Is this not the very height of folly? To succeed well in all other affairs, and in order to gain this success, to allow oneself no peace, no rest; to be in continual agitation, to lose one's sleep, to forget even the necessities of life, and then to fail in the affair which is one's only real affair of eternal salvation, because one would not attend to it, even for a single quarter of an hour: answer me sincerely, Is not this

acting like a fool? What a piteous things to see so many in the world, who call themselves wise, acting with such folly! Do not deceive yourself; that man alone is truly wise who labours unceasingly to save his soul.

3. There never was a case of madness more evident, never a more arrant fool, than he who, in cool blood, puts himself to death, who wilfully drowns himself, or throws himself down a precipice: and is not this what that man does who damns himself? This last case of madness surpasses in extravagance the other, as much as the loss of the soul is greater than the loss of the body. Oh! how many fools are there in the world! The Holy Spirit says the number of them is infinite: and will this folly be less deplorable because it is so common? Do *you* choose to be of the little number of the wise, by devoting yourself, through the whole course of your life, to the most important affair of your salvation. Never lose sight of your end, or you run the risk of not reaching it; never

make a choice to the prejudice of your eternal salvation. This is wisdom. Would you wish to have acted otherwise at the point of death? No, certainly. Then begin this moment to be wise for your own good.

Fruit.—Imprint deeply this maxim in your heart: *That man alone is wise who continually labours for his own salvation.* Repeat it to yourself, impress it also upon others. Never undertake anything without first reflecting whether it will be serviceable for your salvation. If you perceive that it will be a hindrance to you, turn from it at any cost. What consolation will it give one at the point of death and for all eternity, to have been prudent and wise about everything else, and then to be damned?

MAXIM V.

The number is small of those who are saved.

1. Among all the truths of our religion, there is not one which is more

terrifying, nor more clearly demon-
stated than this. How many pro-
phecies, how many figures, how many
examples are there in holy Scripture,
to prove that they are few who are
saved! Our Saviour himself says,
many are called, but of these many
few are chosen. Terrible truth! yet
what effect has it on me? If it were
true that out of 10,000 persons one
only was to be damned, I yet ought
to fear and tremble lest I should be
that unhappy one. Oh! perhaps, out
of so many, few will be saved; and
I live in such security, so indifferent about my salvation! I fear that
of all those who live at present on the
earth, few, very few, will be saved;
the greater part will make a fatal shipwreck, and I live secure, and take so
little pains about the great work of
salvation. Who has told me that I
shall not be of the number of those
unhappy souls which are lost?

2. There are but two roads to go to
heaven—innocence and penance. Is
the number very great of those pure

souls which never have been stained with grievous sin, whose innocence has never been damaged, and those who, after having had the misfortune to fall into grievous sin, do penance truly and savingly? Will these be very numerous? Corruption of morals extends to all ages, young and old. Sin has inundated all the earth. How many are the real penitents, and how many are the sinners? There is no one secure of his penance, and will it be surprising if few gain salvation? The wonder is how a Christian can believe such things, and yet live in such strange insensibility concerning his salvation. People give it no thought. What, then, do they think about it, if they do not think of eternity. Have I sinned? Yes, I am sure of that. Why, then, do I not have recourse to penance? The one only chance which remains for my salvation . . . . Do I believe the words of Jesus Christ; and how can I believe them and not fear? How can I fear, and be so careless about my eternal doom?

3. If Jesus Christ had said that all Christians should be saved, and had said this as distinctly as he has said that the elect will be few, that the road which leads to heaven is strait and the gate narrow; should we live with such unconcernedness about the affair of our salvation?   It is agreed that the road which leads to heaven is the observance of the Gospel, and that there is but one Gospel.   Now, are there many who go by this road—who live according to the maxims of the Gospel? How many followers has the world? People run in crowds where the multitude runs, and yet they know that the multitude runs down the precipice. There is not one of those who have been saved but has walked by the narrow way of the Gospel.   Has Jesus Christ taught any other road? has any other been discovered? No; and, therefore, so few are saved: because so few are those who regulate their life by the maxims of the Gospel—who form their character on the teachings of Jesus Christ.   Am I one of the many who

choose to live after the fashion, and are ashamed to appear Christians? This day, this moment, declare that you choose to belong to Jesus Christ.

Fruit.—The number of the elect is small: be of this number you; aye, and at any cost. You will be remarked, perhaps even laughed at; say boldly, *One cannot do too much for his salvation.* The majority is lost; take good care not to follow the majority. Begin, this very day, to strip yourself of certain ornaments that are too worldly, of certain pastimes little suitable to a Christian, of certain associations far from innocent. Be extremely exact in the discharge of your duties, do not omit good works, and have extreme delicacy of conscience. This is a sure way of getting among the small number of the elect.

MAXIM VI.

Shall *I* be saved?

Reflections.

1. Shall I have the happiness to be of the number of the elect, or shall I have to be among the reprobate? I know not. It is certain there is no middle way between these two extremes. If God is not my eternal happiness, the loss of God will be my eternal misfortune. This alternative is terrible, and makes us understand the necessity of salvation. Meantime, it is hidden from man what shall be his lot, and yet man, a Christian man, in this frightful uncertainty, lives at ease in a state of sin. What unheard of extravagance is this ! Do you wish to know what will be your eternal lot? Ask the question of your habits; examine your life. This and these can answer you whether you will be saved. Question your conscience, and judge by its answers what you will

be for all eternity; but if they should forbode to you eternal damnation, delay not a moment to reform your life.

2. A' life with little that is Christian about it, and which is even disorderly, will this be followed by a holy death? A life formed all upon the maxims of the world; a life given to vanity, to pleasure, to licentiousness, can that possibly lead to heaven? Heaven, into which nothing unclean enters, will that be the eternal abode of a soul all carnal, and will a blessed eternity be the reward of a life of sin? What sort of life is yours? You know, very well, that according to your works God will institute your trial at the last day. You know that the rule of your works has to be the Gospel of Jesus Christ. You are not ignorant of the duties which this Gospel enjoins you—of the precepts it lays on you, to mortify your passions, to do penance, to forgive injuries, to hate the world. It is already a long time since you made profession of the faith and law of Jesus Christ, and yet his precepts are the last you think of

in regulating your actions. Your conscience reproaches you for your irregularities; your heart upbraids you with your habitual disobedience to the divine law. These things are so many witnesses against you, which you cannot escape from nor contradict. What sentence do you expect from the divine Judge? Do you flatter yourself with the prospect of a happy end, of a blessed lot? You would not die as you are at present? You would think your damnation sure. If you do not correct yourself to-day, perhaps to-morrow you will be worse.

3. Piety in appearance only, want of devotion so perceptible, a most feeble appearance of religion—can these persuade you that you will be saved? You do not live even as a Christian; can you reasonably expect to die a saint? What acts of religion do you perform through the whole day? How much time do you devote to the affair of your salvation? Your prayers continually distracted; most rare, very rare visits to the church, and these without devotion,

without propriety of behaviour; confessions without amendment, communions without fruit, exercises of piety without merit—for hypocrisy—for custom; a faith languid and wavering, a charity dead, or almost dead; say sincerely, does all this promise you the attainment of salvation? The frequent want of fidelity to grace, that habitual contempt of the voice of our Lord, those sinful habits, those continual relapses, that fund of cupidity, pride, ambition; these form nothing less than a sensible presage of your eternal damnation. Ah! now, for pity's sake, do not be the worker of your own eternal ruin. Take such steps that these reflections may not be useless to you. Would you wish for a happy prognostic of your eternal bliss? Begin now to live as a true Christian.

Fruit.—Whatever condition you are in you have duties to fulfil, and perfection to gain. Begin this moment to conduct yourself in such a way, that every action may give you reason to trust that you will be saved; frequent the sacraments, which are the fountains of grace and salvation, but do it with due dispositions; entertain a tender and persevering devotion to the Blessed Virgin Mary, and you will have in this a mark of predestination; every day devoutly recite the Salve Regina, to beg of this loving mother the salvation of your soul.

MAXIM VII.

It is impossible to be saved by following the maxims of the world.

Reflections.

1. The world which is condemned by Jesus Christ, is composed of reprobates, has the devil for its prince, is the enemy of Christianity, hates Jesus Christ, his spirit and his maxims, and the Saviour of men does not chose that it should have any part in his prayers—*non pro mundo rogo* (I pray not for the world). This is the world which the same Redeemer has conquered, and has put to confusion, by his cross; this is the world of which all the saints have declared

themselves enemies, and which has per-
secuted all the saints. It is evident
that being of this world is to be of the
number of the reprobate; that loving it,
and following its maxims, is the same
thing as to declare oneself the enemy
of God. God has laid on no one the
obligation to quit the world in order to
embrace the religious state, but there
is an indispensable obligation for any
one who wishes himself to be saved
to follow the maxims of Jesus Christ,
which are so contrary to the maxims of
the world. To gain salvation in the
world, it is of necessity to renounce its
spirit. Has there ever been found a
single worldling, who, at the end of his
life, when people form a sound judgment of things, has been pleased at having followed the maxims of the world?
It is a thing acknowledged as impossible
for one to be saved who leads a life
altogether worldly; and yet how many
make profession in the midst of the
world of following the maxims of the
Gospel! To observe how the greater
part of Christians live, we should say

that the maxims of the world have supplanted those of Christ, so little are they known, so little relished, so little adopted : and what a strange contradiction is this between people's conduct and their faith ! Are you, perhaps, of that number? What confidence can you have, living thus, of gaining salvation?

2. We must come to the resolution either to abandon the maxims and the spirit of the world, or to abandon the maxims of the Gospel and the spirit of Jesus Christ. There is no middle way between these extremes; to attempt to make them agree is madness. Let a man say he is a Christian as much as he will; let him assist at the divine mysteries; if he follows the maxims of the world, he cannot be a disciple of Jesus Christ. The opposition between the one and the other is too great. Jesus Christ condemns ambition, avarice, pursuits of interest, the love of pleasure; what else is there which the world approves? what is there but this which it honours, which it enjoins on its followers? where does it place all

its happiness, but in gratifying such passions? Make these sentiments, if you can, agree with the oracles of Jesus Christ! Jesus Christ commands humility, modesty, self-denial, the carriage of the cross, simplicity, regularity of habits, penance; do they really now-a-days believe in the world that these are the real oracles of Jesus Christ? To see how worldlings deride, mock, insult, make game of one who makes profession of poverty and penance, who lives by rule, who, despising luxury and vanity, professes humility and Christian modesty; one might doubt whether there be any faith left in the world: and is it possible to have a well-founded hope of salvation while following maxims so opposed to the Gospel, so clearly condemned by religion?

3. Reason itself disproves and condemns the maxims of the world—*While we are living in the world we must do as others do.* This is the language of worldlings: and what does it mean? That we must allow ourselves to be dragged along by the crowd

with our eyes shut, without caring to know whither we are going, although it is all the while clear enough, if we would think, that we are on the way to be lost.   Now, to speak honestly, is it acting as people of sense to follow such guides?   Who, with sound understanding, could approve of one giving himself up to the caprice or passions of another? and if you would blame another for doing so, why do you do it yourself ?   If others go to ruin, if others throw themselves down a precipice, what imprudence, what extravagance in you to follow a crowd of people determined on their own destruction!   Yet this is just the meaning of the ridiculous maxim which is so common in the world in our days— *We must do like others*, that is, we must quietly go to hell as others do. We must have no religion except for custom, because it is respectable—for hypocrisy.   We must give ourselves up to our own desires, to our passions, to our appetites, because others do so. We must pass our days in deep forgetfulness of God and of salvation. We must go to hell because others do. Can anything be more absurd ? Can a man of sense, can a Christian, speak more like a fool ? The saints certainly did not think thus, and no one can with-reason say they were wrong. If you follow a line of action like theirs, you may safely promise yourself an eternal destiny like theirs. And will it be wise to lose heaven rather than renounce the foolish and ridiculous maxims of the world? Ah! my God, let not these reflections one day have to be my condemnation.

Fruit.—Conceive this very day a great horror for the maxims of the world, and renew the renunciation which you made of the world in your baptism. Make the holy resolution, act as others who are truly Christian and exemplary. You will find a few of these, and you will find them in every condition. Propose to yourself as your patterns those who are the most perfect, the best regulated, the most devout. There is no more effectual way to become a saint, than to imitate the saints, and to follow the maxims of the saints, which are exactly the maxims of Jesus Christ.

MAXIM VIII.

It costs us more to be lost than it does to be saved.

Reflections.

1. It costs a great deal to gain salvation. The Gospel is rough and hard. The way to heaven is impracticable. This is the common language of worldly people in judging of Christian life; they consult nothing but their senses and their passions. Modesty, humility, penance, displease the senses and disgust the passions; and for that reason, if their voice is heard, nothing is made much of but the difficulties of salvation: but let us consult reason, consult faith, and we shall find this idea to be false. Sinners suffer more to be lost than the servants of God do to be saved. Sinners expect all their happiness from the world which they serve, and from the passions which they gratify; but what slavery can be more hard than

that of the world! How many annoy-
ances, how many afflictions, how much
bitterness, does a wordling experience
in one day, which a servant of God
never meets with in the whole course
of his life! What violence to one's
self, what torment, what cruel vexations, even in the midst of amusements! Slavish, unhappy people,
wretched people, banqueting days,
days of pastime, of pleasure, are the
very days which torment the most
with their bitterness the heart of the
wretched worldling; while the true
servants of God, in their mortification,
in their tears, in their solitude, in their
estrangement from the world, discover
springs of peace, of tranquillity, of
unspeakable sweetness—the sweetness
of the service they render to God,
makes them taste the sweetness of a
Master whom they serve. If you have
had the happiness of loving and serving and being faithful to God one
single day, say with sincerity, whether,
in the midst of the pleasures of the
world, you have ever experienced the

sweetness with which our Lord then refreshed you.

2. It is said that in order to be saved we must keep up a perpetual war against our own passions, and that this is an unsupportable burden. Thus speak cowardly souls, souls which are contaminated; but let people understand what it means to mortify the passions. It means to fight against the most savage of enemies, the most cruel tyrants, of the heart of man; it means not to degrade ourselves so far as to become slaves of the most shameful humiliating appetites. Ask the sinner if, in gratifying his most enticing passions, he ever enjoyed a day of true peace and of real satisfaction; if in suffering himself to be dragged along by his brutish desires, he has ever experienced a moment, even one moment, of true joy. Penetrate into his heart, and you will find there a fund of inquietude and disgust; of fears, of jealousies, of alarms, and what is more than all, unceasing remorse, which torments him unmercifully, and is enough

to embitter his brightest days. It is true he dissembles all this; but will that be enough to render the interior afflictions of his heart less sensible to him? The servants of God have made themselves a rule never to gratify their passions. This is an arduous rule, which obliges them to be always at war with the flesh, which never ceases to attack and to give them battle; they feel all the weight of this cruel conflict, but they have the secret of making it not only meritorious, but sweet and delightful. The hope of being one day crowned in heaven, is enough to sweeten all the bitterness of their interior wars. The sight of the reward which awaits them, after having been faithful to God, overspreads their entire life with such sweetness, fills their heart with such joy, that they would not exchange their condition with the most prosperous of worldlings. You see how cheaply God is served, and salvation gained. Is the cost to be compared with the endless afflictions which sinners have to suffer in order to be lost?

3. Listen to the fatal confession which has to be made in hell by worldlings, by men of pleasure, by the slaves of their passions. *Erravimus a via veritatis.* We wretches have gone astray; we have given ourselves up to our own desires; we have gratified our senses; we have followed the spirit of the world; we have been damned, and O, how much it has cost us! *Lassati sumus in via iniquitatis.* We have wearied ourselves; we have exhausted our strength; we have killed ourselves in order to be lost! *Ambulavimus vias difficiles.* We have chosen to follow the widest ways of licentiousness, the most attractive flowery paths of pleasure; but how many punctures of cruel thorns have torn our hearts on every side! What afflictions in our soul, what violences, what bondage; what fantastic imaginations in the world; what bitter anguish, in order to gratify the whims of some, to comply with the dispositions of others! Ah! fools that we have been, at so dear a cost we purchased for ourselves damnation.

This is what sinners say in hell. Say now, if there has been a religious, a penitent, a hermit, who has led a life more full of bitterness than this; say, if the most fervent servants of God have ever suffered so much vexation and torment in the most rigorous exercises of penance, than sinners have suffered to be lost; and will you be such a fool as to prefer the tyrannical, cruel slavery of the world, to the most sweet yoke of Christ—to the most easy service of God? Will you be such an enemy to yourself, as to chose for yourself eternal damnation at so dear a rate, while salvation costs so little?

Fruit.—Take good care not to be alarmed by those words *mortification, the cross, penance;* the grace of God can sweeten everything. Do not wonder if your senses shrink—do not listen to the empty fears of self-love. Undertake the practice of Christian virtues with great courage, full of confidence in the goodness of the Master whom you serve. In the power of

divine grace, maintain the resolution
to serve your God faithfully till death.

MAXIM IX.

God should be preferred to everything.

Reflections.

1. God is our Creator, our Sovereign Master, our Father, our King,
our Judge: he created us for himself;
we owe to him all we have and all we
are; our eternal happiness or misery
depends on him. What do you think;
does not this God deserve our preference? And yet, when we see the
little care that is taken to please God—
when we see how little account is
made of displeasing him, would there
not be reason to say, that this God
is looked upon by men as a nothing?
Strange thing! people are more on
their guard how they behave with
a parent, with a friend, with a servant, than how they treat God. Tell
the truth, how many times has a
trifling inclination, a little sordid gain,

a ridiculous point of human respect, a brutish indulgence, gained this preference in your heart? What a sad thing to be obliged to make this confession! but, after all, though you should not speak the word, your own conscience speaks, reproaches, and accuses you. At least, be wise enough to lament having till now despised God, who is your sovereign good, and begin, at length, to have an esteem for him.

2. We are obliged to love God with all our heart and with all our strength; for this reason we must be ready to sacrifice everything for the sake of doing his will, and not displeasing him. This obligation arises from the first of the Commandments. If, then, it is true that we love God, and intend to love him, with our whole heart, ought it to cost us a great effort to sacrifice everything to him? Should it give us much pain to prefer his love to every other profane attachment? Once that we know and confess that we are obliged to love God above all things, ought we

any more to hesitate at sacrificing to him some gain, some friendship, some passion, which steals away our heart? "*But this thing is dear to us, it is useful, it is painful to part from it.*" What a wretched difficulty! This proves well how languid your faith is. So we see that a wretched, created good, is more dear to you than God, the Author of all good. Good God! what an indignity—what an injustice, that you will not sacrifice yourself, or that you do it grudgingly and unwillingly!

What a shame—what a want of religion, that a Christian should have need of no end of arguments, of express commands, even of threats, to oblige him to make a sacrifice to God of that which he forbids; to oblige him not to prefer a creature to the Creator—to God! Is it any wonder that few are saved, since so few care enough for God, to prefer him to that which is most worthless?

3. In preferring a creature to God, our heart is guilty of a sort of idolatry.

Can there be conceived injustice or impiety greater than this? What indignation and horror do we feel against the ungrateful Jews, preferring Barabbas to the Saviour of the world—you who profess to know and to adore him, when you prefer to him a fancy, a wretched little gain, a shameful passion? The light of reason alone shows us the enormous injustice of this preference. What! God put in competition with the creature! Faith, good sense, conscience, all rebel against such an impiety; nevertheless, this cause comes to be tried before the tribunal of your heart, and God almost always loses it. Can a greater indignity be conceived in a Christian, who is enlightened with the knowledge of his religion? Can such doings as these be compatible with the faith which we profess? Ah! enter into yourself, and cancel this your impiety by penance.

Fruit.—Jesus Christ has given for you even his own life: what sacrifice have you made up to this time? How many times have you turned from God, from his service, from his love, rather than make a sacrifice of a gratification of your own   Examine seriously to-day in what points it is that you have most frequently preferred the creature to what you owe to God, and make a strong resolution to sacrifice all, even life itself, sooner than fail in your fidelity to God, sooner than offend his infinite majesty.   Accustom yourself every day to make a sacrifice to our Lord of some little gratification, a word, a bit of curiosity, a look, or the like.   This practice will help to keep you always far from preferring any created thing to God.

MAXIM X.

There is no real evil on earth excepting sin.

Reflections.

1. Sin alone deprives us of every good.   The loss of riches, of honour, of health, misfortunes, persecutions, fatal accidents, and death itself, are

called evils, cost many sighs, many tears, cause many afflictions; yet, to speak properly, what evil is there in all these things, if they are not able to take from us a single degree of grace, to deprive us of the friendship of God for a single moment, to rob us of peace of heart or tranquillity of conscience? nay, they may contribute to make us happy, because they can help in making us saints. It is sin alone which makes men unhappy; sin alone deprives a man in a moment of the most sweet joy, of the most tranquil repose which the soul possessed in its innocence. Sin alone robs it in an instant of the grace of God, of his friendship; strips it of all its merits, all its justice, all the sanctity which it had acquired with such efforts. Suppose a man had lived entire centuries in the exercise of the most austere penance, of the most heroic virtues, though he had converted the whole universe, and, moreover, worked miracles, a single mortal sin destroys the whole in an instant; in a moment he falls into disgrace with God, he loses the privilege of being his son, he becomes horrible in his eyes; and if he dies in that sin, he is for all eternity doomed to be the object of his wrath and vengeance. It is then the truth, that sin is the only real evil, and yet, good God! sin delights, sin is loved, and it seems as if nothing could be relished if not seasoned with sin. Have you such an idea as this of sin? have you a horror for it? Ah! that facility with which you commit it, proves clearly that you have another idea of sin from this, but this is not the idea that faith gives of it.

2. Sin alone draws with it every evil. All the misfortunes which have happened since the beginning of the world to our days, the deluge of evils which inundates the earth, wars, pestilences, fires, diseases, and that almost infinite multitude of calamities under which we shall groan to the end of ages, are all the effects of sin. Mortal sin alone has caused, and will cause, the eternal damnation of so many souls;

that eternal fire which the wrath of God has kindled in hell, and there keeps alive for ever, is nothing but the penalty of sin. Conceive, if it be possible, from such terrible effects, the malignity of mortal sin. Let a man die poor, despised, unfortunate, he is yet a happy man if he is not in mortal sin; but what is the death of the greatest monarch in the universe, of the happiest man of his age; if he dies in sin, he shall be eternally the most unhappy, the most unfortunate, despairing wretch, because he will be eternally damned. O my God, can such things be believed, and men make themselves so familiar with sin, and commit it, laughing, for a joke, without displeasure, without remorse, and boast and pride themselves for committing it? Are you convinced that sin is a great evil: that it is the one true evil; how, then, will you live a single moment in sin?

3. Sin alone is hated by God. God is an infinite good, and would cease to be God if he did not infinitely hate sin. He is essentially good, and he would

not be so if he did not essentially hate sin. God hates nothing except what is opposed to and offends his infinite goodness. Sin alone is that evil monster which outrages God, which takes arms against God, which rages against God, to destroy him, to drive him from his throne. Conceive, if it be possible, the hatred which God bears to this his enemy, and hence judge of the infinite malice of sin—for a single sin of one moment, God cast into hell an innumerable multitude of angels, creatures so noble, so excellent, so perfect, capable of giving such glory to God, for all eternity. For 6,000 years now God has been taking vengeance on sin. His vengeance, however, is not yet satisfied; it will last as long as the world; the fire of hell will last as long as God. Can any greater evil be discovered; rather, can anything else be truly called evil besides sin. Sin will be for ever the object of God's hatred and wrath; it will be for ever a matter of repentance to you. How is it possible that you are not filled with horror at the very name of sin ? What extravagant folly is this, to believe that sin is the chief of evils, nay the only true evil, and then to love nothing but sin !

Fruit.—Conceive so great a horror for sin, that you may be ready to lose every thing, life itself, sooner than commit it. Repeat continually with sincerity of heart, *O my God, sooner die than offend thee.* Do not be content with having a horror for sin, have it equally for the occasions of sin; fly from these as from sin itself. A man does not sincerely detest sin, if he does not fly from the occasions of it. Endeavour to inspire others also with the like horror. How many families would live innocently, if parents betimes inspired their children with a horror for sin !

MAXIM XI.

There is no state so horrible, nor so unhappy, as that of a soul in mortal sin.

Reflections.

1. A soul in the state of sin is an object of horror in the eyes of God. Man, who is created after the image and likeness of God, by sin is so deformed, that the lines of the divine likeness are so disfigured, that God knows it no more except as an object of horror. The man may be surfeited with honours and pleasures; he may have arrived at the summit of greatness; he may be seated on a throne; if he is living in a state of mortal sin, he is more horrible in the eyes of God than a stinking corpse is in the eyes of man; all the treasures of the universe, all the riches, all the luxuries, all the pomp and greatness of the world, do not prevent the sinner who continues in his guilt being abominable in the eyes of God. Yet people live with tranquillity in that

state; they take delight in being in it, and it gives them displeasure to leave it. You who could not endure to have on your face for one day a spot of dirt, you have been carrying sin in your soul for years and years, sin which makes you so horrible in the sight of God. Have you ever understood the terrible unhappiness of this state? have you ever thought what it means to be an abomination before God? If you have, how can you live thus tranquil? why do you not wash away with tears that most foul stain of your soul, and return through penance to the friend-ship of God?

2. A man in the state of mortal sin is the object of the anger and indig-nation of God. If the wrath of God does not break out upon the sinner, it is purely the effect of his mercy. If this mercy did not put a check on the fury of all creatures, and on the malice of all the devils, do you think sin-ners would survive the moment when they fall into mortal sin? All creatures would rush upon them to slay them,

and avenge the outrage done to their Creator. How many fatal accidents, how many unforeseen strokes, how many sudden deaths are seen, every day, to cut short the life of sinners, in the very flower of their days! These are all effects of the wrath of God. The real cause of the greater part of the misfortunes with which men are afflicted and scourged, is not understood. It will be understood one day; and it will be seen that these were chastisements from the hand of God, in anger with sinners. Men sin, they live in sin, and then they wonder that such a family is ruined, that such a city is laid waste, that such a one has been brought to beggary, such another has been killed; the wonder should be how the earth can support sinners who live in sin, who are pursued at every moment by the terrible wrath of God, as objects of his anger. You may escape from the anger and wrath of a prince of this world; but how and where will you escape from the wrath of an Almighty God, of a God who is your enemy: and if he strike you with death in the state of sin, O God! . . . .

3. A man in the state of mortal sin, is a man in disgrace with God; he is a criminal condemned to the extremity of punishment. Consider the sad loss which a man incurs by sinning. He loses the grace which made him the friend of God, he is stripped of all merit before God, fallen from all the advantages and privileges which the state of grace conferred upon him. Would there be imagined a more unhappy condition on the earth? Oh! how well have the saints known this truth! How much have they not done and suffered to escape falling into this extreme misfortune! To escape being separated from God, honours, pleasures, treasures, persecutions, tortures, death itself—nothing would move their constancy; they sacrificed all sooner than lose that divine grace which you care for so little, that you give it up for a nothing, and when it is lost, are so careless in recovering it. O my God,

the Christian knows all the while in what a lamentable state he is living if he lives in sin; he knows that if he dies in that state, hell is his habitation for ever, eternal fire is his inheritance, the torments of hell his portion; he believes this, and yet one moment after another he lives in sin. There is something here past understanding, but experience proves it a real case.

Fruit.—If you have the misfortune to be in the state of mortal sin, have recourse at once to the sacrament of penance. Gain the habit of examining your conscience every day, and practising frequent acts of contrition. Not only take care not to omit duties of obligation while you are in sin, and the other exercises of piety which before you were accustomed to, but practise fresh good works, so as to move the infinite mercy of God to grant you the grace of a sincere and durable conversion.

MAXIM XII.

There is nothing more dangerous for a soul than the delay of conversion.

Reflections.

1. I have need to be converted. I would not wish to die before this work is done. The bare thought of this misfortune, of this danger, terrifies me. What! To die without being reconciled to God—without having made that restitution which I am bound to—without having reformed my bad habits? Ah! I should be damned. What reason, then, have I to put off my conversion to another time? What is more uncertain than time? Although I should not delay my conversion beyond one single day, who has told me that I shall have that day to be converted in? Who can give me security that this one day shall be mine? What extravagant folly! for a man to risk his soul, his salvation, on the most uncertain day of his life—on a time of which he is perfectly aware he cannot

dispose! How many persons have been taken off by death on the very eve of the day of their intended conversion! Oh! what a calamity, to die with nothing but the project of a future conversion! . . . Good God! what joy will be mine to-morrow, the day after, and all the days of my life, if I am converted to-day! . . Yes, this day may be the last day of my life; it may also be the day of my salvation, if with all my heart I return to God. Shall I choose to continue any longer the greatest enemy of my own happiness? Shall I choose to live under the risk of damnation?

2. Suppose you knew that there will be time for you to be converted— the supposition means nothing; the thing is uncertain; but never mind— suppose it was certain that there would be time, the question rises, shall you be converted? Perhaps you will never think of it again, if you are not converted to-day. In order to be converted, it is not enough to have the time, there must be *the will*—there

must be *grace*. Who has told you that, when that day comes until which you have put off your conversion, you will have a better disposition for it than you have at present? Shall you be more convinced then than you are now of the extreme necessity in which you are of being converted? . . . Now you are thinking about it, you are reflecting on it, you understand this truth, and yet you will not resolve. *One may be converted any time* you say. But who has told you that at any time you will be in the state to be converted? You have refused to be so when God was moving you, when the obstacles were not so great, the ties not so strong, your bad habits weaker; can you reasonably hope that you will have the will when the obstacles will be increased, your bad habits will have become inveterate, and your inclinations to evil stronger? If you are not converted to-day, you run the risk of never being converted. Will you then be such a fool as to delay your conversion any longer?

3. Although you should, at that future time, have the mind to be converted, by what revelation are you assured of thus having a more efficacious grace than that which you have hitherto resisted ?   Our Lord gives you means now, which, perhaps, he will never give you again.   The feelings which you now have, the meditation which you are now making, the stings which now touch your heart, if you resist them now, will, perhaps, never return. God now offers you his friendship—he offers you his grace, and you are not pleased to accept it at present; and by your acts you say you will not have it, you do not find it convenient to break off that habit, to quit that company; in short, now, you will not be converted. After so offensive a repulse, do you expect that God will keep his friendship in store for you against a future time ? Would you yourself act thus with one of the meanest of your fellow-creatures? It is an astounding thing that such reasonings should be necessary to per-

suade a Christian to be converted; that means to persuade him to come out of the present danger of being damned. You fear, perhaps, that it is too soon to begin to-day to do penance, to hate sin, to love God. You fear it is being too much in a hurry to cease being a sinner, being one of the impious, if you ceased from it this moment. Ah! if you do not cease to-day, if you are not converted now, perhaps you will never be. Make your resolution.

Fruit.—You know to-day that you have need to be converted. Delay not till to-morrow: have the consolation before the close of this day of seeing it done. Examine, before the crucifix, the points of your conversion. In what respects had you to be converted? What bad habits had you to reform? What passion had you to subdue? What have you to correct in your words, in your actions, in your amusements? Put nothing off till to-morrow. To-day let your reformation give a proof that your conversion has taken place.

MAXIM XIII.

It is real wisdom to despise the world, and not to fear its judgments.

Reflections.

1. People have immense consideration for the world. Day and night they study how to please the world. They fear nothing so much as to displease it: to the world they sacrifice their happiness, their rest, their very soul. For fear of the world and its judgment, they put off their conversion, and come to die without being converted. Everything has to be regulated according to the views of the world, everything must be made to square with its maxims, its ways. *The world will have it so. The world does not allow this. What will the world say?* This is the language we hear continually. Good God! how disgraceful that such language should be heard among Christians! What is this world which is so esteemed, so counted

on, so feared? What right has it to impose upon us such hard laws? even forbidding us to return to God? Now do you know what is this world which Jesus Christ has condemned? It is a mass of vain, turbulent people, who do not like the maxims of the Gospel, who have no rule to guide them but their passions, who have no object for ·their love but earth and filth, whose entire business is pleasures, tricks, deceit. It is a crowd of godless, irreligious, corrupt souls. Such is the world. Such is the master, whose slave you become, by thus fearing its judgments, respecting its maxims, obeying its laws. Can there be greater folly than this? to allow the world to exercise its dominion over the soul, to keep command over the heart: and ought we not to be indignant with ourselves for having paid it such regard till now, and been for so long a time deceived by it? The saints alone have been truly wise, who have despised and trampled on the world.

2. No master can be harder, more

cruel and ungrateful, than the world. What does it not exact of all those who serve and love it? labours, punctuality, the most servile dependence, a slavish servitude, a most painful violence upon ourselves. And after all these pains and labours, what reward? After you have undergone the most distressing fatigues, if the enterprise does not succeed, all your fatigues go for nothing. You may have passed whole years of suffering to bring to a successful issue some undertaking, to fulfil some employment, which the world laid on you: has any one sympathised in your sufferings—any one assisted your exertions? Has any one expressed any satisfaction at your anxious diligence? A single mistake is enough to make the world laugh at and despise you. What sort of a master is this, who takes no account of the good will of his servants, who judges of the merit of an action only by its success, and who has no recompense to offer but contempt, mockery, endless vexations and bitterness, and an eternity of punishment in hell? Such is the world. And is it possible that Christians, possessed of good sense, should love, value, and fear this godless world? Is it possible that they should make themselves the slaves of this cruel tyrant? What weakness, what folly is yours, to serve a master so unworthy to command you, who can do nothing for you but make you miserable! What extravagance to prefer the love and esteem of the world to the love and service of God! Are we, then, any longer to leave it in doubt whether we will despise the world and give ourselves to God? This surely is true wisdom.

3. What is there in the world to deserve all this regard and love? Greatness, honour, dignities, titles, riches, pleasures: behold here the good things of the world. Now, have these things ever yet been able fully to satisfy a heart? Has the man ever been found, will a single man ever be found, whose heart has been or will

be full, whose desires satisfied, whose longings brought to an end by the goods of the world? Ask the question of those who are considered the most happy in the world, and they will tell you that the goods of this world have nothing real and solid about them except the most cruel afflictions, which they occasion and which they purchase. What is more inconsistent, vain, and fleeting than the goods of this world? Will it, then, be wise to build our expectations on that which will vanish in a moment, to fix the heart on that which is no sooner gained than lost—the pleasures of the world, which are so greedily sought for, and which the world promises to all so liberally. What are they? They are an inexhaustible source of bitterness and disquietude; they are a perennial fountain of displeasures and regrets. Let a man dissemble his feelings as he may, let him put on a cheerful countenance, get up artificial smiles, the interior disgust with which worldly pleasures are accompanied spreads

through the soul, and cruelly torments
it. Good God! what sweetness can
pleasures have of which infallibly we
must repent! You are stupid, you are
senseless, if already knowing this truth
by experience, that in the world there
is no real good, you still love the
world, serve the world, and cling so
tenaciously to the world, that you
cannot resolve to despise it in order to
be converted to God. The goods of
this world are no goods except to
those who despise them, and trample
them under foot for the love of God.

Fruit.—Declare yourself the enemy
of the world; make yourself a law
always to have a horror for its spirit,
to despise its customs, its judgments,
and its maxims. Keep far from
those assemblies, from those conversa-
tions in which the spirit of the world
rules—luxury, vanity, fashions. The
pomps of the world are not things to
have possession of your heart. Trample all these things generously under
your feet. If you do not despise the
world and its false goods, you will

become its slave, and make your whole life miserable. Judge of the world now, as you will judge of it at the moment of death.

MAXIM XIV.

The yoke of Jesus Christ is sweet, and his burden is light.

Reflections.

1. The yoke of Jesus Christ or the service of God is not accompanied with those severities, those violences, those bitternesses, which we fancy; it is sweet, charming, and light. Let a man be once converted, once given up to God without reserve; let him love God sincerely; then, whatever he will do for God will be easy and sweet. Those souls which have generously despised the world, which have chosen the service of God as their only portion of the world, which have abandoned themselves into his hands, and having stripped themselves of everything, desire nothing but what he

desires—what peace, what interior joy, what sweetness, do they not experience! Bearing the yoke of Christ implies some sacrifices, but they are voluntary sacrifices, which are prompted by a loving heart, and therefore are sweet. In the service of God there are sufferings; but one chooses to suffer, he loves to suffer, and he prefers suffering to all the false delights of the world, the mere seeing of himself free from the fears and the tyrannical desires of the world, from the slavery of the passions, from the cruel remorse inseparable from sinful pleasures. Good God! what sweetness does this not spread through the heart! This alone makes the yoke of Jesus Christ sweet and light. But worldlings do not believe this. It cannot be believed until it has been tasted. How comes it that you, too, do not believe it? It comes from your not choosing to be converted truly to God, and to practise what Jesus Christ commands; and then you complain after that, that the world which you serve tyrannizes over you and oppresses you. Begin now to serve God, take upon you the yoke of Jesus Christ, and you will know by experience how sweet and charming it is.

2. The present life has no sweetness nor delight, which is pure, except in carrying the yoke of Jesus Christ and serving God. Every other state of life is filled with vexation, confusion, bitterness. The master whom we serve is the God of sweetness. He knows how to sweeten his yoke with a secret unction, and to inundate the souls which serve him with such delight and joy, that they will even lovingly complain of the excess of their consolations. When will worldlings—those unhappy slaves of the world—have to complain of too great consolation, of over much sweetness. The joys of the world are all superficial; they cannot reach the heart except to torment it. Jesus Christ imposes laws, but these are different from the laws of the world, inasmuch as they are not hard to any but those

who will not observe them. The spring of all our afflictions are our passions. Jesus Christ, by his Gospel, teaches us to repress, to obtain, to subdue these merciless enemies. What man can be happier than he who is free from the tyranny of his passions? It is true that the way of the Lord has crosses, but the fruit which these produce has an exquisite sweetness, because the testimony of a good conscience and unchangeable peace of heart are the dearest delights of one who serves God, and bears the yoke of Jesus Christ. Hence come those tears of consolation which the servants of God shed at times at the foot of the crucifix, where they find a pleasure more pure and more exquisite than will ever be found in the world. You do not understand these spiritual delights. The yoke of the Lord appears to you bitter and severe. The bitterness and severity is not in the yoke; it is in your own badly-disposed heart. The burden of the law of God is easy and sweet. Do you wish to prove by experience this truth of our faith? Give up the service and love of the world, and give yourself sincerely to love and serve God.

3. There is nothing in the world concerning which people form ideas more false than concerning the yoke of Jesus Christ and the service of God. People come to represent it to themselves as an impassable country, full of monsters. We should say that each one takes a delight in forming a frightful idea of it; but which shall we listen to, our own passions, our own self-love, or Jesus Christ? He tells us that his yoke is easy and his burden light. Who is deceived? All the saints. All those who have borne it tell us that it is sweet, and that its sweetness cannot be described. Surely these have not all combined together to deceive us. That would be saying too much; therefore it is we who deceive ourselves. Ah! what do you fear? Is it that God does not know how to sweeten his yoke with the interior consolations of his grace? This is a deceit. Or that

he cannot render lovely the most austere practices of penance? An error again. Be converted to God—abandon yourself to God—leave the rest to him. It is enough that you should love Jesus Christ, to experience sweetness in the difficulties in his service. You will suffer; but you will suffer with joy, with peace and consolation. You will fight; but you will gain the victory, and God will crown you with his own hands. You will weep; but your tears will be sweet. Love Jesus Christ, and this love will console you in your troubles, will sweeten your crosses, will set you clear from all that it is dangerous to love, and will give you a disgust for all false pleasures of the world. This love will change all your evils into good; will make you despise the world and its vanities; will make you know, by a sweet experience, how lovely is his yoke—how delightful it is to serve God.

Fruit.—Choose to-day to serve God alone, to bear faithfully the yoke of Jesus Christ, observing his law with exactitude, and it will not be long before you will taste its sweetness.· He asks nothing extraordinary of you —prayer, occupations, common obligations of a Christian, duties of your state. This is what he exacts. Neglect nothing; fulfil everything with diligence and from a motive of religion, and you will find everything easy and agreeable. Displeasures and irksomeness in the practices of devotion generally are the effect of being faithful by halves, of a heart divided between the world and God. Remember always that you were not created to serve and love the world, but to serve and love God.

MAXIM XV.

Unless you do penance, you shall all perish.

Reflections.

1. Consider that this declaration is infallible. Universally, and without exception, the necessity of penance is

indispensable; no age, no condition, no rank is exempted from it, whether you be the great ones of the world, the happy people of the age, nourished with delight, brought up in delicacies and luxuries, worldly women who have lived in idleness and vanity, men of business, merchants, men of letters—if you will not do penance, you will all perish. Whether they be nobles or plebeians, young or old, poor or rich, there is no salvation to be hoped for them without penance; even those who live in misery, are obliged to do penance to be saved. In vain a man may labour, suffer, weary himself for the whole course of his life; if he does not suffer in the spirit of penance, it is all in vain. Useless troubles, barren sufferings, cares thrown away—without penance, no salvation. We may discuss the matter as long as we please, make subtle distinctions, explanations, interpretations; this is an oracle which cannot be eluded—it is a sentence clear and distinct, the sense of which cannot be darkened. Wherever you are, if you cannot do penance in proportion to your sins and to your wants—sincere and persevering penance—you will perish. Understand the force and sense of this oracle. Why such great dread of penance? Do you prefer to perish for ever to submitting to a short penance, which will open heaven to you?

2. Either you are a sinner or you are innocent. If you have not sinned, you are capable of sinning; and this is enough to make penance indispensable. Innocence! Ah! innocence is a precious treasure which we carry in earthen vessels. A multitude of enemies, crafty and watchful, are always seeking to rob us of this treasure! Our own heart is often our most dangerous enemy. Our inclinations to evil are continual and violent. Everything is temptation; there is war on every side. The very air we breath is contagious. Everywhere we meet with snares and dangers. If we wish not to fall—if we wish not to be

conquered, we must have preserva-
tives; we must have armour. Penance
and mortification is necessary. We
must bring down this body of sin;
mortify these senses, our enemies; subdue this rebellious flesh; tame these
insidious passions. You will not long
preserve innocence without the help
of penance; and if you have sinned,
do you dare to expect forgiveness
without penance? All the pains of
hell are not punishment too heavy for
one mortal sin; and you, stained as
you are with thousands of enormous
sins, do you expect to gain pardon
without penance? What madness!
There is no third way for one who
has sinned: hell or penance. Unde-
ceive yourself; every sin must be
punished, either by an avenging God,
or by the penitent man.

3. What penance has not Jesus
Christ himself done for having taken
on himself only the likeness of a sinner? The most innocent saints have
passed their days in frightful austerities. For the most trifling sins, they

have condemned themselves to most severe penances, to continual tears, to the hardest fasts. We do not profess another religion from theirs. Have we sinned? Our conscience answers yes. And what is our penance? There is no one who does not hope for the same happiness as the saints enjoy—who does not look for the same crown. Now, on what is this confidence founded? On the merits of Jesus Christ you will say. No doubt, it is to his merits we are indebted for our salvation; but will they avail us without penance? The same Jesus Christ says, No; *unless you do penance, you will all perish.* He was not ignorant of the value of his blood—of the efficacy and price of his merits; yet, with all this over-abundant redemption—with the fruit of his passion so full, no one will be saved, says the Saviour, if he does not do penance. Heaven and earth will pass away, but the words of Jesus Christ will never pass away. This single sentence, well pondered, is enough to make you become a true penitent. What will it profit to know yourself to be a sinner, if you do not do penance?

Fruit.—Let the first penance be that of the heart. Begin by a lively and sincere sorrow, by repentance, and by bitterness of heart, with which you may detest your sins. Besides this, exterior penance is necessary to mortify and humble the body. Do not omit the penances commanded—abstinences of obligation, the fasts of the Church; add to these voluntary mortifications. It is a good penance to suffer insults, contradictions, cutting words, with patience and in silence. Do not give ear to your own delicacy, but to your conscience and your necessities. Mortify your senses and your passions; let mortification be your ordinary virtue. Never forget *that it is infallibly necessary that we should perish, if we do not penance.*

MAXIM XVI.

Virtue and sanctity are easy for every one.

Reflections.

1. Virtue, in whatever state we may be, and under whatever aspect we view it, is amiable. This is its character: meekness is its constant companion; sincerity, good faith, modesty, charity, justice, whatever deserves honour and respect, all enter into the portrait of virtue. Now, what difficulty is there in being a man of good faith, in being an upright, sincere man, a man of modest deportment? What difficulty in being an affable, gentle, charitable man, in satisfying the obligations of our state? But virtue, it is said, is situated upon a high mountain. True; but how easily may this be climbed— how easily God may make plain the way! A little labour is necessary. That we do not deny; but this is abundantly recompensed as soon as the object is gained. What sweetness,

what peace, what tranquillity, what serenity reigns on that mountain! Oh! how well is one rewarded for the toil undergone! One never suffers so much to be virtuous, as one must inevitably suffer to be at liberty and profligate. Worldlings confess that a good man is happy. They envy his tranquillity, they admire his unchangeable peace; and when they come to die, they would wish to be in his case; but still they like better to die with a desperate regret at not having been virtuous—at not having become saints —when they might so easily have done it. Will you, too, be so foolish as to run yourself into this misfortune?

2. God has given the commandment to every one to be perfect, as our Father in heaven is; but with infinite goodness he has made the sanctity and the perfection of each to depend on the performance of the duties of the state of life to which he belongs. Could he condescend more to every condition of men—could he make the task more easy? What excuse will

there be for those also who live in the
world, if they do not become saints?
People fancy that sanctity is confined
in cloisters, or buried in deserts or in
caverns of the mountains. It is an
illusion; it is a deceit.   Sanctity is
within the reach of every one. Christian virtue springs up on every soil;
and if this most sweet fruit is not
everywhere produced, it is the fault of
the cultivator. Many wish to serve
God differently from what he requires;
many others will not serve him faithfully in that which he commands.
This is the reason why sanctity, which
belongs to every state, is gained by
very few. In the great variety of states
in which men live, the observance of
the commandments, innocence, mortification, and all Christian virtues,
suitable for every kind of person, *good
works are necessary*.   How many of
these may be done without going out
of your own house, or your own employment! *Crosses are necessary for
entering heaven!*   God has scattered
these, and has distributed them in abun-

dance among all conditions of life; nothing is wanting but to make agood use of them. We have need of graces and helps. In what plenty does not God furnish every one with these? All that is wanted is, that we correspond with them. With what ease may you become a saint; but if you do not, what will be your desperation to have seen and known all this, and not to have turned it to account!

3. What a consolation is it to find that virtue and sanctity is a thing so easy to attain in our own condition of life, at our own age, in our own rank! With a little exactitude, fervour, and fidelity in fulfilling our own particular duties, great sanctity may be gained. It may be, fulfilling your obligations costs you a deal of toil; but would it not, perhaps, cause more if you neglected them? What afflictions, what uneasiness, what displeasures, what remorse do those wilfully bring upon themselves, who do not choose to lead a life suitable to the character of a Christian. On the con-

trary, what pleasure and joy is found in fulfilling exactly the duties of one's own state! However little a man may possess of honour, of religion, and good sense, is there any one so dull as not to be able to relish the sweetness of a good conscience? The secret tortures which larcerate the heart of libertines and bad Christians, form the finest eulogium of the virtues of the good. In vain do profligates dissemble their feelings, and put on a forced artificial cheerfulness. The virtuous man alone possesses real interior joy. Let the world say what it pleases, it costs more, it is more difficult, and harder to be a godless man, than it costs to be a saint. Only make the trial, and you will be fully convinced of this truth.

Fruit.—Apply yourself seriously to acquire the virtues proper to your state, and to satisfy all your duties. Neglect none of them. Take pains every day to correct some defect, and to grow more devout. Do not be discouraged by the first difficulties at the beginning. This earnest application, this violence to yourself, is a little disagreeable, but as you go on it becomes a sweet pleasure. If you have a real zeal to save your soul, the difficulties all vanish. The struggle is but short, the fruit of the victory eternal.

MAXIM XVII.

Time is precious; the loss of it is irreparable.

Reflections.

1. Nothing is so precious as the time of this life. There is not one moment which is not worth an eternity. Eternal happiness, the unspeakable glory of the blessed, is the reward of making a good use of time. Time is so precious that all the honours, all the riches of the world, are not worth so much as one moment is worth. If a man had employed but one moment to gain the whole world, if he has not gained heaven he has lost all his time. There is not one man among the

damned who would not be ready to give all the goods of the world, if they were his own, to have one moment of that time which he has lost, and of which we make such little account. In every instant of time a new degree of glory may be merited; and this is what the blessed in heaven will not be able to do for all eternity, with all the acts of their superior virtue. In one moment I can, with one tear, with one sigh, appease the wrath of God, and obtain the pardon of my sins. This is what the reprobate will never be able to do, by suffering the most frightful torments of hell. Our salvation can be gained only during time, and there are persons who aim at nothing but to pass and consume this time. Good God! what an afflicting thing, what despair will there be when death comes, to see that time is all gone by, and that time is all lost! Unhappy me, if I do not now make good use of that time, which one day I shall have uselessly to regret.

2. There is no loss in this life more

irreparable than the loss of time. For
every other loss there can be found a
remedy. If we lose our health we
may recover it: we lose a lawsuit, lose
a battle, lose our reputation; some
piece of business goes wrong; we may
hope for a remedy; there is a chance
to ward off the evil consequences. If
all other means fail, we may have recourse to supernatural, miraculous aids.
The loss of time is the only loss which
cannot be recovered, nor remedied.
God himself cannot order that the last
past day should not be past; that all
the years which have been spent in
idleness, in vanity and pleasure, should
not be lost. Time past by will never
more return; and whatever portion
of it you have not employed for your
salvation is lost irremediably. You
will be able to employ better the days
which yet remain to you, but you will
not be able to repair those which you
have lost. O God, what a loss!
We are passing the time! That is
what people say about the time which
is lost in vanity, in games, in amuse-

ments not fitting a Christian, in parties of pleasure. Good God! how little does such language suit Christian lips! This time which you have passed, in other words, which you have miserably lost, will it ever come back? Will it be possible to recover it? What, then, all the time of my infancy lost for ever! those beautiful days of my youth irreparably lost! Of all the days which I have hitherto lived, how many can I call full days—days well employed for my salvation? On what have I spent, on what am I spending all my time? that time which was given me for no other purpose, but to carry on the all-important affair of my eternal salvation!

3. The loss of time is of extreme importance. How many graces destined, prepared, and attached to those days, which you have misspent, have been lost with them! Perhaps on those days depended your conversion; perhaps the grace of vocation, or of perseverance. God was then calling, inviting, moving. There was

then leisure at your command, opportunity for reflection—in short, you had time. It is passed, it is lost, and you are not converted; you are not become holy, and perhaps will have no more time for it. Oh, how important will the loss of time appear to us when we come to die! Oh, we then shall say, if I had but one hour now of the time which I have misspent! Oh, if, instead of wasting my days in sensual indulgences, in pastimes, games, and idleness, I had employed at least one half hour in meditating on eternal truths, in taking care of my soul! I have lost all my time, and I die. What despair! All this time will be required of me by the Sovereign Judge, who gave it me, that I might spend it to advantage for the life to come. What shall I answer? What a terribly strict account I shall have to render! What eternal anguish is before me! Is the importance of this loss known? If it is known, how is it that people suffer it without remorse, with satisfaction, laughing, and as if they would be sorry

not to suffer it? Are you a Christian?
Are youi n your senses? Why, then,
be guilty of an excessive folly, which
must be followed by regrets the most
cruel, but most hopeless? Why squander thus time which is so precious, and
squander it irreparably?

Fruit.—Time is precious . . . time is
short: the loss of time is irreparable.
Reflect often on these three truths.
Do not lose even a moment of your
time. When you make your morning
prayer, consider the value of the day
which you are beginning, and which
may perhaps be your last. Promise
our Lord that you will pass it all in a
holy manner. Never be idle. Do not
fail to accuse yourself in all your confessions of the time you have lost.

MAXIM XVIII.

I must die, but I know not when.

Reflections.

1. It is certain that I have to die:
but when shall I die? Will it be soon,

or will it be late? I do not know.
Thus far I am sure, that this day may
be the last of my life. The Son of Man
will come in the hour when he is least
expected. Whom have you ever seen
die who did not promise himself to
live at least till the next day ? What
folly is this ! People know that death
is certain, and may seize us at any moment; and yet they look on it always
as a thing far off. Of all those whose
death you have heard of during the
last year, was there even one, think
you, who expected to die within the
year? No one can assure me that I
shall be alive to-morrow. This is as
much as to say that I may die to-day.
But this day, which is to decide my
lot, the last of my life, will it be to
me the beginning of a happy eternity?
This single question puts me into confusion; this thought, by itself, terrifies
my conscience. Ah! what would become of me, if, within an hour, I had
to appear before God, to render an
account of the time I have lost, of the
graces which I have abused ? What

would become of me, if, loaded as I am with sins, without having done penance, I should have to go in a few minutes to hear and to undergo the last sentence? The case may happen —it has happened again and again; it happens every day: where is my security?

2. To believe that we may die any hour, any moment, and not to fear and not to watch, this can only be impiety or madness. Can it be that a man condemned to death by an unchangeable sentence, unless he has lost his understanding, will give himself up to pleasures, to mirth, and think of nothing but enjoying life? Good God! the sentence is already pronounced against all men, that they must once die: we know not when the moment will be on which our eternal doom depends; and yet no one thinks of it. As if dying well were an easy thing, and dying ill were a matter of no consequence, we live, without reflection, in a state of sin. If I knew for certain that to-morrow I should

die, I should prepare for it to-day. Ah! perhaps it will happen yet sooner. I may die this very evening—I may die this very moment, while thinking of it. If this happened, should I be prepared? How should I? It is certain that those who have thought the most on death, shall yet be taken unawares. What will become of those who do not think of it, who even are determined not to think of it? How strange it is! Men are full of precautions and forethought concerning the interest of this world, to ensure a happy conclusion of their affairs; and as for their eternal salvation, as for their soul, as for ensuring to themselves a good death, they think it lost time to employ one moment about them! Little hope is there of a holy death for you, if this is the way in which you act.

3. Consider how great is the happiness of those faithful servants, whom the Master, when he comes, shall find watching. What joy to the Saviour of the world to gather in their persons

the fruit of his toils, of his blood-shedding, and to be able to pour forth on them the torrents of his blessings, when receiving them into paradise! and what delight for those faithful servants that they did not fall asleep, as so many others! What joy that they never lost sight of the affair of their salvation; that they lived an innocent life, with the thought of death always before the eyes of their mind! With what gladness do they welcome the moment which is to decide their eternal lot. Good God! what a difference between the just man expiring, and all the falsely happy ones of the world when they die! How many, so to say, sleep through the whole course of their life, and how terrible is the thought of not awakening up till death comes! Under what a mistake, in what danger have you lived till now, if you have lived without being ready at every moment to appear before the Sovereign Judge! Where should you be now, if he had called you before his tribunal? Do you intend to spend your whole life thus?

Fruit.—Do not forget, as often as ever you approach the sacraments, to dispose yourself as if it were the last time in your life that you were to receive them. A confession made as if it were the last, a communion received as if it were the Viaticum, cannot but be efficacious. This pious practice is one of great advantage; but do not follow it only when you receive the sacraments. Accustom yourself to do nothing in your life without taking a view of it, as it were, from the point of death. Whether it be the choice of a state of life, or any other matter of importance, if you wish not to make mistakes, try all things by the test of death. Form your judgment of all things, as you will judge of them at the point of death.

MAXIM XIX.

It is great imprudence—it is the height of misfortune, to meet death unprepared.

Reflections.

1. The necessity of preparing for death is absolute. Nothing is of so great importance as death. Nothing is so difficult as to die well, especially for one who has not made preparation for it during life. If nothing were wanted to constitute a good death, but to receive the last sacraments, to kiss the crucifix, even to shed a tear or two, our imprudence in not preparing for that great step would not be so insufferable. It is not always difficult to find a confessor, to receive the Viaticum, and the other consolations of religion; but how many, with all these helps, have yet died in sin! To die with a crucifix in one's hand, to die surrounded by priests, to make an edifying death, this is all very good; but a holy death does not precisely consist in this. To make a good death, is to

die after having cancelled all the disorders of our life; it is to die in
the state of grace; to die with love
towards God, such as surpasses every
other love. Now, this is not so easy
a matter for one who has passed
through his whole life without thinking of dying well. There is nothing
to which Jesus Christ has so earnestly
exhorted us to pay attention, as to
this preparation. There is no one
who will not agree, that to die well
we must prepare to die. There is
nothing so alarming as an unprepared
death. Yet, after all, what does this
alarm avail? If you were to die
this moment, have you nothing to
fear? What imprudence, to hazard so
thoughtlessly a trial of this consequence! You think, perhaps, to make
your preparation when that last hour
is come. You will not make it, and
you will die unhappily.

2. If we had to die twice it would
be a case of less imprudence to risk
dying badly once: you might repair
the mistake. But we are to die but

once, and a happy or unhappy eternity depends absolutely on this one death. Once that you have died badly, the evil is without remedy. Strange inconsistency! One has to make his appearance in a theatre, in a pulpit; one has to undergo some trial of talent or of learning. Months are spent, nay, entire years, in making preparation, although the result signifies little, and the effects of a failure may be recovered from. Good God! how much time is taken during life to prepare for death, though the entire life ought to be engaged in this one thing? The saints, after spending all their life in fasts, in prayers, in tears, removed from all intercourse with the world, buried in solitudes to prepare for a good death, were in fears and doubts concerning that great passage, while we, who live in complete forgetfulness of death, caring for nothing but to pass our days in pleasure, quietly expect to die a Christian death! We hope to be prepared for death, and to die well, without having ever thought of it!

Extravagant folly is this! It is no wonder that so many Christians die ill, as they have never learned to die well.

3. Conceive, if it be possible, the horror, the agitation, the despair of a soul, at the moment when called to appear before God, when not expecting so soon the coming of the Sovereign Judge. The past, the present, the future, are all frightful at that moment. Grievous sins not expiated, restitutions delayed, projects of conversion put off to a later day, all the movements of grace smothered; all these come in a troop to crush and torment the poor soul with a thousand troubles. How terrible to see oneself in the hour of death with such reasons for alarm! What imprudence to wait for that critical hour to make one's preparation, and what a misfortune to be arrived at that hour unprepared! There is no putting off the hearing of our cause to another court day. No delay is allowed. The Master is come, and all is found in frightful confusion. Shall we, then, dare to say we had no

time to prepare in? Think of all the time wasted in chimerical schemes, in vanities, in doing nothing. What a surprise, what horror, what desolation, to have to appear before God to render in our accounts, and the accounts not ready, and nothing done to gain favour with the Judge! If only I had been ignorant of the danger of being thus taken unawares—but no, I knew it, I believed it, I have thought of it, but all without fruit. What will then become of me? I am going on the way to meet this misfortune, if I do not prepare for death.

Fruit.—The best preparation for death is a holy life. This is a preparation about which the whole of life ought to be engaged. Ask yourself every evening what progress you have made, what preparation for death. Gain the habit of performing all your actions as preparations for death. Masses, prayers, practices of piety, duties of your state, sacraments, all should help towards a good death. Besides this general preparation, fix

upon a day every year to be consecrated entirely to this great affair of
preparing for a good death. On that
day regulate your devotions so as all
to be as though preparatory for near
approaching death. Still better would
be the practice of employing in this
way one day in every month, and even
every week. Whatever degree of
care you take to ensure a good death,
you will never do too much.

MAXIM XX.

Death is sweet to the just.

Reflections.

1. Everything combines to render
the death of the just sweet and precious. The remembrance of the past
inundates their soul with the most
sweet delight. A melancholy exile
coming to an end, a succession of evils
brought to a close, an alternation of
tempests, fears, and dangers passing
away, a stream of disquietudes and
troubles, which is now dried up for

ever, a happiness pure, full satiating,
now beginning. Let us understand,
if we can, what a fund of interior
consolation is here for a Christian living a holy life. What joy must a
good man experience at the hour of
death, when reflecting on having
spent his time well, on having corresponded with graces, made good use
of the sacraments, controlled his passions, and lived in the practice of
virtue and penance! If he found
anything in the service of God painful, all is now passed—fasts, humilia-
tions, toils, austerities, mortifications,
all at an end. What a joy, then, that
he did not do the evil which he might
have done, and that he did do the
good which he was obliged to do!
How can he now help rejoicing that
he did not follow the maxims of the
world, that he did not take part in its
profane delights, in its poisoned pleasures? What would remain to me
now, says the happy dying man, of
all these things, but bitter regrets?
Oh, how charming it is at that moment

to be free from such remorse, and to have nothing but the consoling testimony of a conscience well at rest! Death cannot but be joyful when one dies a saint. But are you likely to die a saint, if your life is not even that of a Christian?

2. The prospect of the future no less contributes to sweeten the death of the just man, and to fill his soul with inexpressible joy, a foretaste of eternal happiness. The sight of an angry God is precisely that which makes death horrible. But there can be no fear of falling into the hands of this God if you have loved him; do now love him, and have the most consoling assurance of being tenderly loved by him. The thought alone that he is dying only to live for ever, and that this eternal life begins at the moment of death, what delight does it not pour into the heart of the just man dying! How does it sweeten all the pains of his present condition! He experiences now a depth of confidence in the mercy of God, to whom he

ascribes all the good he has done, which makes all his fears vanish away, and makes him hope that neither temptations, nor troubles, nor all the snares of hell, will be able to separate him from God, and prevent his attainment of a blessed eternity. What joy, what ineffable peace is then his! We can never know the worth and fulness of it but by experience. Good God! what a difference there is between the death of the wicked and of the just. But strange as it may be, all would wish to die the death of the just; all admire and envy the death of saints; but when will people begin to follow their example? You will not have much satisfaction when you come to die at having desired their end without ever undertaking to imitate their life. You must not expect to share in their joy at the hour of death, if now you do not share in their penance and their sanctity. They would never have come to so sweet a death if they had not been saints, and you have no right to expect it, living as you do.

3. The reflections of a good man dying, after leading a Christian life, make the most sweet impression on his spirit, and spread through his soul a peace and consolation, which are superior to the senses, and cannot be understood by a carnal man. What would it avail me at the present time, says the dying just man, to have amassed great riches, to have been raised to the first honours, borne the first offices of state, enjoyed all the pleasures of the world? What would all this profit me, if I had not gained salvation? Oh! how wise have I been to have despised in time what I shall condemn for ever! These are consoling thoughts indeed. The choice was before me, he goes on, between a happy and a miserable eternity. My salvation was the one affair which I had to mind. I have been in danger of losing it. If I had not secured it, what despair should I be suffering now! but, by the grace of my God, I see myself now near to the blessed country. I have had to labour for it, to struggle,

to fight; but at length I have succeeded. What a consoling thought is
this! What a pleasure will it be at
that day to think over the sufferings
and the toils gone through during life
for the love of God. I see, he says,
multitudes who have made a miserable
shipwreck, and are eternally lost; and
I am come to the port. I am saved.
Imagine to yourself, if it be possible,
a joy more pure, more solid, a sweeter
consolation. Will it be your lot to die
in this manner? Take care that these
most salutary reflections may not be
barren for you. Let not your having
had them now put before you be a
fresh cause of affliction for you at the
point of death.

Fruit.—A man's death corresponds
with his life. What will give consolation and peace when death comes, is
a life led like a Christian. This is the
time to make the resolution, that, by
the grace of God, you will gain for
yourself a holy death by a good life.
Say to yourself often what S. Bernard
used to say: *We must die the death of*

the just; but for this end we must live like the just. Every morning, when you wake, say, like S. Teresa: *Here is another day given me to merit a blessed eternity and to prepare for death. Will this death be holy? I must have it so at all costs.*

MAXIM XXI.

Death is terrible and frightful to the sinner.

Reflections.

1. *The death of the wicked is very evil,* says the Holy Spirit. The deepest, most cruel afflictions come crowding to torture the heart of the dying sinner. The approach of death, the memory of the past, the view of his present state, the fear of the future, all combine to terrify, to crush, to throw him into despair. *We must die.* It is inevitable; there is no escape. This sentence is terrible to a man who has never thought of death without horror. *We must die*—that is, we must leave

our riches, we must bid adieu to all
the pleasures of life, we must quit the
world, which is the idol of our affections, we must go to appear before
God to be judged. How many things
have we to bear; how many things
draw tears from our eyes; how many
things there are to be done; how many
things there are to be feared, and
there is but one moment for all this!
We see everything prepared for our
trial; we have the proofs of our guilt
in our own hearts. God is on the
point of pronouncing judgment. Sin,
which once appeared so attractive, is
now changed into a savage monster,
into a cruel tyrant, against the dying
sinner, and comes to attack, to torment,
and torture him. Oh! death of the
wicked, how terrible thou art! Thou
art in thyself a hell. This is all simple
truth; and yet sinners are to be found
on earth, and I myself, perhaps, am
one of them.

2. The confusion and the horror
into which the soul of the dying sinner is thrown by the remorse of his

guilty conscience at that moment, become his punishment. It is now he feels all the load of sin—now he sees through the sense of these things. In death there are no more unbelievers—no more libertines; faith revives—the strongest passions are quelled—truth is seen in its clearest light. Men know feelingly then, that God was the end for which they lived on the earth ; that God ought to be the one object of our love and worship. What an affliction to have served any or every other lord but him; to have loved any other good, to have followed any other guide besides God! What a great consolation would it be for me, will say the sinner in that extremity, if I had passed my days in the service of so good a master! How many times did I feel myself moved to take this course! How many graces were given me, to enable me to do it! How many favours did God confer on me, to constrain me to love him! But I did not choose, I did not please; and now I die! And whom

have I been serving all my days?
What have I gained by serving the
world? Immense troubles, continual
pains, fruitless labours, cruel servitude, a life wasted and thrown away
in bitterness; and now I die! What
recompense have I gained for all
my labours? Behold it here! Tormenting despair, a horrible death now
awaiting me; an unhappy eternity before me; and meantime I die! Good
God! that all this should be believed,
and yet men live, carelessly live, in
sin!

3. The thought which, of all, the
most embitters and tortures the miserable sinner in his death, is to know
that he might so easily have been
saved, and yet is about to be eternally
lost. He will say, I have entirely
neglected my salvation; worldly
business, games, pastimes, pleasures,
shows, have absorbed all my time,
and I have not given one day to my
soul. How often was I invited to it
by some pious book, by some servant
of God, by some preacher! I could

have done it, but I die without having done it, and I die to go and be condemned to eternal flames. Oh, what despair! If, at least, I had been converted a year ago, when I was put into terror by reading about the terrible truths of my faith! I could have been; nothing was more easy; but I did not please to be, and I die with this cruel recollection. I now see that I have had to suffer more living as a libertine licentiously, than I ever should have done leading a Christian life. I now see my folly; I shudder with; fear but there is no more time now to repair my error; and I die! Conceive, if you can, how sad is a death like this. There would be some relief to the poor sinner's mind, if this calamity, these errors, could be attributed to some cause besides himself; but he knows distinctly that he alone and exclusively has been the worker of his own perdition; he sees, and he will see for all eternity, that he is damned for having preferred the heavy tyrannical slavery of the world, to the sweet yoke of Jesus Christ. Ah! for the love, such as it is, which you bear to your own soul, prevent in time, these sorrows, which, when you come to die, will be unavailing, but now might convert you!

Fruit.—Form a correct idea of the extreme danger in which a sinner, who lives on in the habit of sin, is, of making a very evil death. Live innocently, if you do not intend to die in sin. Reflect often on the sorrows which, at the point of death, throw the soul into despair; and do now what you will then wish you had done. Every day ask God, through the merits of the death of Jesus Christ, the grace to die the death of the just, but, at the same time, neglect nothing to secure it for yourself.

MAXIM XXII.

The last day of judgment will be terrible for sinners,
and consoling to the just.

Reflections.

1. What will make the last day of
judgment terrible and dreadful to sinners, will not be so much the frightful
signs which will precede it, as the judgment itself. A rigorous examination
of all the sins of your entire life, from
the first moment when you came to the
use of reason till your last breath—
sins which were forgotten, sins ex-
cused to yourself, sins which you could
hardly perceive, all will be brought to
light. Not the very least fault, not
the most trifling circumstance, the most
subtle hidden motive of your actions,
will escape that examination, nor be
hidden from the eyes of the universe.
Good God! what confusion, what
crushing shame! All the hiding-places
of the conscience will be laid open, all
the mysteries of iniquity brought to

light, all the most disgraceful, most brutish passions, will display themselves in all their malignity to the eyes of all men. Who will be able to endure to make so hideous an appearance? But it cannot be avoided. In this life the sinner has but a weak, imperfect idea of the malice of sin. On that day he will have a clear and distinct apprehension of all its enormous gravity, of all its horrible malignity, of all its disgusting foulness. This sight by itself will suffice to fill him with anguish, horror, and despair. He will see his enormous ingratitude in repaying with sins the infinite mercy of God; the outrageous contempt with which he treated his ineffable majesty, when he sinned; the monstrous abuse of his infinite goodness, which his sins involved. Conceive, if possible, the confusion, rage, revenge, grief, torment, which this sight will cause to the sinner. Conceive what the terrors of that day will be to you, also, who are making this meditation, if you do not change your life.

2. The examination will be followed by the sentence of the Divine Judge. After the sentence will come the separation between the reprobate and the elect; the former being condemned, as wretched victims of divine justice, to the eternal flames of hell. What torment, rage, and despair will that terrible sentence, that eternal separation, cause to miserable sinners: *Go far from me, ye cursed.* It is a God who speaks thus, in a tone the most tremendous—a God who drives the reprobate for ever from his lovely presence; and whither, Lord, are they to go? To eternal fire, to burn and blaze for evermore in hell. That is the sentence definitive, without appeal, immutable. Good God! how terrible, how frightful is this sentence! What despair will it strike into unhappy sinners! Mingled with a countless crowd of pagans, Turks, heretics, miscreants, the wretches will go headlong into the infernal abyss, while the elect will spring up triumphantly to glory. Ah! with what good reason, yet with

what fury, will the reprobate then say, as they are being parted from the elect : Fools that we were! Their life appeared to us madness, and their end without honour. We despised their poverty; we mocked at their modesty; we laughed at their tears; and yet we see them now reigning for ever in heaven. We, then, have been deceived; we, then, are condemned; for us there is no escape, no mercy. And these terrible truths are believed by sinners. Oh! how horrible it is to confess we have gone astray, when we are already falling down the precipice, and there is no remedy. What will be the sentence pronounced on you at that day? Think well of it now, and provide in time for your eternal welfare.

3. Far different will be the lot of the just on that final day, when the sound of the angels' trumpets shall call the dead to appear before the tribunal of God. They will hasten with joy and gladness to come forth from their tombs, to receive their

Judge and Father, who is soon to crown them with glory. What feelings of love and joy must overflow their hearts at seeing themselves called out from the crowd of the damned, and placed on the right of the Redeemer. Oh! how will they rejoice then at having loved him, at having followed his maxims, at having suffered for his love, at having always preferred his love to all things besides! How will they look now upon the reprobate, upon those great ones of the world, who had so little Christianity about them; those libertines; those worldly women, nourished up in delicacy and vanity; those who pretended to be the happy ones of the world, now doomed with the wicked to eternal flames! Oh! how will they congratulate themselves for having chosen the right side, for having been prudent, and not allowed themselves to be seduced by the snares of the world! Shall you be of this happy number? But what will complete the happiness of the elect, will be the loving invitation by which the Divine Judge, with a look most amiable, will introduce them into the heavenly kingdom. *Come, O ye blessed of my Father, to possess the kingdom which has been prepared for you.* What delight, what joy will those most sweet words cause to their hearts! Behold us, they will say, in a rapture of wonder—behold us, after our short toils, made heirs of God himself, heirs of an eternal bliss. Can there be conceived a more happy lot, more consoling joy? and can there be folly more extravagant than to take the utmost pains to be deprived of this lot, and to fall into the irreparable misfortune of the reprobate.

Fruit.—Keep always before your minds the day of final judgment. This was what S. Jerome did. If you wish to meet with the mercy of God in that terrible day, judge yourself now without mercy; examine yourself for confession with great exactitude and with great severity, but avoid the mistake of those who give all their attention to examining their conscience, and none to the detestation of their sins. Do not excuse yourself, do not flatter yourself, do not cover your sins, because they will then be laid open to your confusion at the day of judgment. Gain the habit of examining your conscience every evening, and many times in the day besides, and thus anticipate the judgment of God. This practice is of great efficacy to keep you far from sin.

MAXIM XXIII.

The greatest of all misfortunes is to be damned.

Reflections.

1. There is a hell, that is, a place in which the omnipotence of God combines all sorts of torments to punish and to inflict suffering on those who die in sin, and to make them suffer for ever; a collection, a reunion, a heaping together of all evils, and of all evils in an extreme degree—pains

without intermission, sorrows without
end, regrets without bounds, an endless duration, an infinite eternity of
punishment. This is hell. And yet
hell is something more horrible and
more frightful than all this. Conceive
the misfortune that it is to fall into
hell. There the wrath of a God taking
vengeance for the outrages committed
against him, kindles a fire, the heat and
activity of which are beyond compre-
hension, and which contains in itself
every kind of torment. There the
damned is sunk, buried, drowned in
that fire. He is immoveable in that fire
like a rock; he is penetrated by it like
a hot coal; he can breathe nothing but
that fire which burns him. He burns,
he rages madly, he despairs; his suffering is continual, and he always has
before his mind the thought that he is
suffering without end and without
relief.   Oh! what a misfortune to
suffer at every moment a fire which
devours but does not consume, torments without destroying; to suffer all
imaginable torments, to suffer them all

at once at every moment, to suffer them without relief, to suffer them for eternity! There is a hell and there are sinners! There is a hell and you sin! and you continue to live a single moment in sin, and you travel on, laughing, to hell!

2. To burn in hell for as many years as we have lived days, would be duration of pain to strike us through with horror—a misfortune to terrify and astound us! What will it be, then, to burn in a lake of fire, in a sea of torments, for as many millions of ages as there are drops of water in all the rivers and seas of the world? And yet one of the damned shall have suffered in that prison of fire for all this inconceivable extent of time, and yet not one moment of his eternity will be passed. The end of ages will have buried the whole universe in its own ashes. After the end of the world there will have run out as many millions of ages as the world has lasted moments, as there are grains of sand in the mountains; and nothing of that

frightful eternity will have passed. The damned one will have as much to suffer as if it were the first moment of his hell. O eternity, thou art frightful! thou art incomprehensible! And there are Christians who believe in thee and sin! This is not less incomprehensible than the duration. What sorrow, what desperation, for a soul to suffer in the first moment all that it will have to suffer for an entire miserable eternity! Eternity of sorrows, eternity of sufferings, eternity of despair, eternity of punishments, eternity of hell! The understanding loses itself in this eternity, but the soul of one damned shall never lose one moment of that eternity. He will never be able to say to himself—*there remains to me one-quarter of an hour less to suffer.* After a thousand millions of ages of torments, he will not be able to say—*one hour of my sufferings is over.* No, never. The torments of the damned are always present, and nothing ever passess of what is eternal. To burn always, to burn for eternity, and to be certain of burning for eternity, there is his lot, there is the sum of his misfortunes. O my God, people believe in the eternity of hell, and they run joyfully, and for mere sport, down that horrible precipice! We have either lost our faith or we have lost our senses.

3. Hell, with all its torments, would be no longer hell, if God were not lost in hell. This irretrievable eternal loss of God is infinitely more cruel a woe than all the punishments of hell. This is properly the hell of hell. This constitutes the sovereign calamity of man. We must understand what God is, in order to conceive what it is to lose him, and to lose him without the hope of ever recovering the loss. Man has been created for nothing but for God. This is his end, his happiness, his centre; conceive what it is to lose that for the love, enjoyment, and possession of which we were created; to lose the sovereign good, the fountain of all happiness; to lose God, to be hated and reprobated by God for ever, to be the

fatal object of his eternal wrath. What thunderbolt could there be more stunning, more destroying, fraught with more despair, than to see oneself rejected by God—than to hear the words addressed to oneself: I know you not; I never will know you; you shall be for ever an object of horror to my eyes; for ever the object of my wrath: no more compassion for you; no more recovery for you; you shall never more see my face for eternity. Good God! and is it possible that men think it nothing to lose thee? The saints tremble with horror at the bare thought of the possibility of losing God, because they knew what a sad misfortune was this. If you have no horror for sin, if you do not fear to die in sin, you are throwing yourself into the danger of losing God for eternity.

Fruit.—Let the thought of hell become familiar to you. Often reflect on the misfortune of those who, buried in that horrible eternity, have no more hope of the least relief in their sufferings. This practice will be most useful to you for escaping from hell, and for living a Christian life. When tempted, when in danger of sinning, recall to your memory the idea of a miserable eternity, and say to yourself: *I do not choose, for a few moments of pleasure, to purchase to myself an eternity of pains, and to lose God.*

MAXIM XXIV.

The damned will be continually tormented at heart with most cruel anguish, but all to no profit.

Reflections.

1. However terrible and incomprehensible may be the sensible pains of a damned soul, we may say that all this is but little in comparison of the agonising sorrows, the feelings of eternal despair, which this one reflection causes him: *I have lost God for ever; and I have lost him for nothing.* I am damned, says a reprobate; I have lost an eternity of

happiness, a paradise of delights, a glory without end, because I have lost God for ever, without remedy, without hope of recovering him for eternity.   What anguish, what rage, what remorse, what despair must this crushing reflection cause in a damned soul! I have lost God, and in losing him I have lost all, because I have lost the origin of all good, out of whom there can exist no good.   I have lost God, who was my last end, the most amiable of all fathers, the most sweet of all friends, the most magnificent of all kings.   This God whom I have lost looks on me no longer as his son, no longer as his friend, no longer as his subject, but as a rebel against him. He sees in me nothing but a being hateful in his eyes, condemned for all eternity to be the victim of his wrath. If there were but some way to remedy this loss.   But no, says the damned soul, I have lost God for ever; I shall never see God more for eternity; I shall never more for eternity love God, never more for eternity shall I enjoy God. Oh! what terrible torment does it bring to the heart of the miserable reprobate, that he has lost God for ever! Do you comprehend the excess of this punishment? and if you comprehend it, how can you find a relish in pleasures? how live on in sin? how delay your repentance?

2. What will make this eternal loss yet more bitter, is the reflection that he has been lost for nothing. If a man had lost God for ever, to gain the whole world or a thousand worlds, the loss would not be less horrible, nor less irreparable; but to reflect that God has been lost for a mere nothing, to satisfy a brutish passion, the doing of which has been followed by so much trouble, to run after a little smoke, an empty toy, a shadow; what indignation against himself, what spite, what rage, to have been so lost to reason, to have been so senseless, as to lose God for ever, for a thing of nought, which passed by like a dream! I am damned, says the reprobate; I have lost my soul, I have lost God: and for what have I

encountered this loss? For a few hours' amusement, for a few instants of insipid pleasures, for a point of human respect, for fear of displeasing some person, for fear of contradicting some libertine. For a nothing I have lost God, I have lost all: I am damned. What affliction will it cause to a soul to reflect on the short continuance, the childishness, the mean, low character of the pleasures for the sake of which he has been damned and has lost God! And what a despair to know the complete inutility of this affliction! to know that for all eternity he will have to be repenting over his perdition! Now I can repent, O my God, with advantage; now I can do penance with fruit. What madness and extravagance would it be to wait till I am in hell, to repent there to no purpose?

3. If a reprobate was able sometimes to forget the subject of his repentance, he would have a torment the less; but he will have it always present to his mind; and the reflections

of his mind will incessantly furnish
his heart with matter for most tormenting and bitter anguish. The understanding of a wretched reprobate
will be a sort of executioner to
him. His mind will be immove-
ably fixed, obliged to attend, without one passing distraction, to the
thought of what it was which turned
him away from God, and made
him miss the attainments of his last
end; always forced to see the error of
his vain fancies, the emptiness of his
pleasures, the wickedness of his desires.
He will make efforts to turn his
imagination from all this; but this continues with more and more clearness
to represent to him the nothingness of
what he is damned for, and thus will
be increasing the torture of his despair.
A hundred times, says the reprobate in
hell, I have condemned the vanity of
the world; yet I did not cease to follow
it, and for its sake I am damned!
How often have I thought about hell!
I believed all I now see and feel, and
yet I am damned. I have raged with

indignation at the thought of men damning themselves for a nothing, yet here I am damned myself for a nothing. I have also foreseen the sorrow I should have for all eternity, if I was damned, and now I have this sorrow, I shall have it for ever, and it will be eternally useless to me. Good God! do we believe these things? If we do, how is it possible we should stupidly forget our future lot? why do we attend to nothing but what is present? why not think in time of preventing the bitter and useless sorrows which are suffered in hell?

Fruit.—God is lost for ever by one mortal sin, if a man dies in that sin. Often recall to your memory this terrible truth in the midst of all your affairs, during all your actions. Renew often in the day this resolution, *rather to sacrifice all things, rather to lose my life, than be separated from God.* This practice will be effectual to keep you constantly in the grace of God, particularly in time of temptation. In all accidents of life, if you lose rela-

tions, friends, property, comfort yourself with this thought: *If only I do
not lose God, every other loss is a nothing.
If only I possess God, I have gained all.*

MAXIM XXV.

There is no one damned. who does not certainly know
that his damnation is his own work.

Reflections.

1. To be unhappy by necessity is a
deplorable case; but at least in this
case we cannot reproach ourselves
with our own misfortune, and all the
anger falls on him who was the cause
of it. But to be unhappy in the
highest degree, eternally unhappy, because we have chosen to be so, by our
own sheer wickedness, whereas we
might have been eternally and supremely happy; this is a folly of which
there is no example except in our
damnation. There is no reprobate in
hell who does not see, who is not convinced, that he is eternally miserable,

because he chose to be so, that he is
the worker of his reprobation, whereas
he might have been saved, and that
easily. I am damned, says the reprobate, because I chose to be damned.
It was in my power not to be damned,
and I did not choose to take the means
not to be so. I did not choose to correspond with the grace, with the invi-
tations which I had to be saved. I
had time, I had every convenience
to gain salvation; and yet I chose the
abuse of these for my damnation.
Many and many times I formed the
resolution to obey that commandment,
to forego that pleasure, to be converted
to God; I was able to do it, I had the
inspiration to do it, and yet I did not
do it. Such a man and such another
are saved. It was no interest to them,
more than it was to me, not to be lost.
They had no means to keep out of
hell which I had not. Heaven was
not offered to me at a higher price
than to them; yet they have gained
their salvation, and I have not gained
mine, but am damned. I was destined

for heaven, I have lived in the Church, been nourished with the sacraments, enlightened with faith, supported by grace: I might have been saved; I have chosen to be lost. My God! what cruel affliction, what despair to know that we have laboured for our own ruin, that we owe our damnation to ourselves! Draw advantage now from these reflections, which you will have to be making for all eternity without advantage, if you are damned.

2. The most clear knowledge of the facility with which we might have become saints and been saved, will increase in us, if we are damned, the tormenting conviction that we have wilfully thrown ourselves headlong into hell. What a torment to think for eternity on the multiplicity of help which we had to gain salvation, and not to think of them, except to have always before our eyes, how easily we might have made good use of them, and we did not choose. What would it have cost me, we shall say in hell, to have lived with a little more regu-

larity, to have taken a little more pains to bridle my senses, to mortify my passions? what would it have cost me, will say some libertine, to give up those pleasures which, in themselves, were so bitter to me, to keep from that company, to shun that wicked place? what would it have cost me, will say some rich man, to make that restitution, to forgive that injury, to redeem my sins with alms-giving? what would it have cost me, will say some worldly woman, to have dressed myself with a little more propriety, to have observed a little more modesty in my behaviour, to have kept myself more retired, to have deprived myself of so many vain pastimes, and to have practised a little more devotion? Ah! now the yoke of Jesus Christ appears sweet; his love now seems charming; now it seems an easy thing to serve God. What violence, what struggles, what displeasures have I not gone through to serve the world, to live after my own desires, to satisfy my appetites! It is certain it would not have cost me so much to save myself. In order to be lost, I found it necessary to make an obstinate resistance to the remorses of my conscience, to the lights of reason, to the movements of grace, which I might so easily have seconded, and become a saint, so as to be saved; but I am not saved, I no longer can be saved, and I shall eternally grieve at the thought that I have not chosen to be saved. Thus thinks, thus speaks, thus feels, but all in vain, a damned soul in hell. From these thoughts there then springs a furious hatred against his own free will, burning rage against himself for having caused his own eternal ruin. How many of those who now make these reflections will one day have to speak in this manner! Do not you be such a fool as to be one of them.

3. There is no saint in heaven who does not see, who is not fully convinced that he is indebted for his salvation to nothing but the blood and merits of Jesus Christ. So, likewise, there is not one reprobate in hell who is not convinced that our Divine Sa-

viour has done all to save him; but he, in spite of his grace, of his passion, of his death, has chosen to be damned. He will know that Jesus Christ did not exclude him from the benefit of redemption, that he was born and lived upon earth, suffered and died for him and for his salvation. He, moreover, merited for him, and made over to him, all the graces which were sufficient to make him a saint. He will then remember how many times this Good Shepherd called him, invited him; how often, also, full of solicitude for his good, he held him back when he was going astray in the ways of iniquity; but he would not listen to him, would not correspond with his mercies, would not avail himself of the price of his redemption, would be damned in spite of this most loving Redeemer. O my God, what a torturing grief to think eternally that Jesus Christ gave all his blood for my salvation; to think to what a degree Jesus Christ had loved me, to what an excess his love carried him to purchase Paradise for me, and to think that I have chosen to renounce Paradise; that I am no longer able to love Jesus Christ, that I shall never more be loved by him, and shall be eternally miserable, because I chose to be so. Oh, cruel remembrance! Oh, terrible despair! towards which I am travelling apace if I do not change my life, and reform my ways.

Fruit.—Repeat to yourself when you are tempted: Do I intend to be damned? I can gratify myself, but the fruit of my guilty pleasure will be hell. If I determine to sin, I freely accept the condition of being damned. If Christians would make this truth familiar to them, they would live differently. The saints have taken every care to have it always before them; have a great horror of mortal sin, looking on it as a title-deed which ensures you eternal perdition. Always remember that if you are saved, your salvation will be the work of Jesus Christ; but if you are lost, your damnation will be all your own work.

MAXIM XXVI.

Eternal goods alone are real goods.

Reflections.

1. The goods of this world have nothing solid, real, or satisfying in them.   They are properly nothing but goods seen in a dream; they have no value but in the imagination or the opinions of men.   They cost great labours, great trouble; but, after all this trouble, what, in fact, has been gained?—a name, a shadow, a figure, which passes by.   These goods are unstable, fleeting, transitory, made to be a source of disquietude, uneasiness, fears; made to be the tyrants or the torture of men.   Inquire of those who have the largest share of them, if all this be not true.   There is no other sort of goods belonging to this world. And can a man be called wise who reckons goods of this kind to be real goods, who places his happiness in

them, who spends his life in running after these false goods? Yet they are the idol of worldly people. O my God, when, then, shall we cease being deceived? When shall we be convinced that eternal goods are the only real goods—the only goods which can content the mind, satisfy the heart, meet all our wishes? There is nothing here below which can enable us to understand the ineffable sweetness of possessing eternal goods. A joy, pure and full, an unchangeable calm, perfect satiety ; this is what is experienced by those who enjoy the good things of Paradise. There we shall have all that we desire, because there is nothing more to be desired. The heart is full, the soul is satiated. What the blessed are inundated with is an ocean of pure delights, and the source of all these goods is God himself, who is their possession. This is a weak idea of the goods of Paradise. Are not these worthy to be placed in the balance against the wretched goods of this earth? And is not yours a lamentable case, if, for the sake of acquiring these false goods, you lose the eternal goods of heaven?

2. The possession of created goods creates disgust, and leaves a void in the soul which disquiets it, because all that there is pleasing in them is limited, and no sooner are they gained than they vanish; even if they were less frivolous and superficial, their short continuance is sufficient by itself to make them incapable of satisfying the heart of man. People toil, wear themselves out, to gain the goods of this world; and scarcely is the fruit of their labour brought in, when they die. And what sort of goods are these, which wither in the very bloom of their enjoyment? So it is; the most happy man upon the earth, the richest, the most honourable, he to whom nothing is wanting of all the goods of the world, he is made unhappy and perpetually uneasy by the thought of death, which will take away from him all the goods which he possesses. In heaven a soul lives in perfect happiness; the goods of it are pos-

sessed with the certainty of never losing them for all eternity; and this certainty of their eternity makes them
more sweet and satiating. It is now
six thousand years since the angels
have been in possession of those incomprehensible goods which they contemplate and enjoy at the very fountain
of all good, which is God; and they
contemplate and enjoy them with a
delight which is ever fresh. The world
will come to an end, and thousands
and millions of ages will have passed
after it will have ended, but the goods
of Paradise will never end; the charming possession of them will never cease;
nay, not one moment will have passed
of the eternal happiness which they
afford to a soul which possesses them.
Comprehend, if you can, how consoling, how delicious is this thought. I
am happy, and I shall always be. I
possess God; with him I possess every
good, and I shall possess him always.
My heart floats in a joy pure and perfect, and this joy is never to end. In
short, I am blessed; I am saved, and I

shall be for ever. Good God ! how void of reason, how senseless are we, if we seek after other goods besides those, which can make us happy—that is, eternal goods !

3. Eternal goods are great; they are incomprehensible; but, perhaps, we might say that not less incomprehensible is the indifference of a great part of Christians for these goods which constitute eternal happiness. Created as they are for the eternal enjoyment of the Fountain of all good, born for heaven, called to a heavenly country, what ought to be the force of their desires, what their eagerness for that city of the saints, for the gaining of those imperishable, perfect, and satisfying goods !   Being here on earth in a state of banishment, they should look on its false goods with nothing but contempt; they ought not to love this abode so full of bitterness.   They should rather send forth unceasing sighs towards their blessed country, and look on death as the end of their imprisonment. Thus, in fact, have the

saints thought; thus have they reasoned and acted. Do we think and act thus? Good God! how great is the disorder and unruliness of the heart of man! Every day we see by experience how ungrateful, hard, and unjust the world is, and yet we bind our hearts to it every day more closely. We feel the vanity, the uncertainty, the inconstancy of the false goods, which fill the heart with displeasure and disgust, and yet, by our own choice, we make ourselves their slaves; we are captivated by filth and smoke. O Religion! O Reason! is this all the use we make of your lights? What object can be more worthy of a Christian soul, better able to satisfy our heart, more deserving of our love and our desires, than heaven, than eternal goods? Begin to love them, and you will lose your taste for the goods of the earth.

Fruit.—Heaven is our true country. Its goods are our true riches We are on this earth as pilgrims, as travellers. A traveller does not pay much attention to what is doing in the

country through which he is passing.
The remembrance and the desire of
his country keep him always engaged.
All that the world can present us of
pleasant and enticing should not deceive us.   Look on it all as dirt, as a
shadow passing by.   Look on everything created with the eye of a
stranger, and remember always that
there are no real goods, except the
eternal. If you wish to be less attached to the earth and its false goods,
think often on heaven and its eternal
happiness.

<hr>

MAXIM XXVII.

True joy is not found on earth.

Reflections.

1. There is nothing more common,
more universal on earth, than gladness
and joy, and yet nothing is more rare
than true joy. Everything breathes
gladness; all the world loves gladness; nothing it hates more than sad-

ness. All are continually in search of joy; and to judge by what goes on upon earth, we should say that joy must be the portion of worldlings. But no such thing. The pretended joy and gladness of the world, besides being light, superficial, and insipid, is false in its origin and bitter in its end. Worldly joy usually springs from poisoned sources; and, therefore, instead of quenching thirst, it kills. The gratification of a passion, a party of pleasure, the accomplishment of a desire, the gaining some great dignity, or some distinguished honour, these things produce what is called gladness and joy. But is the heart content? Is the soul in peace? It is not enough that a good thing should please us, it must be in itself a real, solid good, or else the gladness is false. Of all the goods which cause such gladness in the world, there is not one which renders a man happy, which contents and satisfies him. Every one bears thorns of displeasure and remorse; and what sort of joy is it which can be felt in the midst of such bitterness? Innocence alone gives true joy. If the source of the worldling's gladness is vicious, the gladness itself is false, only apparent, artificial. There is laughter in the world, and plenty of it, but it is unnatural and forced, got up on purpose, artificially to hide the interior bitterness which tears the heart. This is the joy of the world. It deserves not the name of joy. What kind of a master, then, is the world, which cannot pay its servants with a little real gladness! and what extravagant folly is yours, if you become the servant of the world, with the sacrifice of your true joy! Serve God, and you will soon find true gladness.

2. It avails a man nothing that others should count him happy and joyful, if he is not so indeed. His own heart, and not the opinion of others, must decide. If the most brilliant feasts, the most sumptuous appearance, the most merry amusements, leave the soul sunk in bitterness and

sorrow, what does it avail to be supposed by others the happiest of men? Now this is what all worldly joys end in: their fruit is most bitter to the heart; they do nothing but make the spirit profoundly wretched. Ask the worldling what has he ever gained from those pleasures, those plays, those parties? Disquietude, melancholy, sadness. Noise and dissipation suspend for a short time these feelings; but no sooner is the noise ended, than the heart returns into itself, and finds there a depth of remorse, troubles, and regrets, which cruelly torture it. What remains to that libertine, to that worldly woman, of all those revellings, all those pastimes, all those boasted joys? Nothing but sorrow at having squandered their time, lost their health and their innocence. What remains to that dying person of all his feasts and his pretended joys? Mortal paleness, bitter tears, which bear witness to the sorrow and sadness of the heart. What remains of all their worldly vanities to the reprobate in hell? If the joys which they felt were any-thing real, innocent, and lawful, wherefore now such cruel regrets?   Why such well-grounded repentance?   O my God, when shall I begin to be wise, and seek real joy in thee only, and in thy love?   This very day—yea, this very moment.

3. Do you wish to know where real joy, real gladness, is to be found? In the hearts of good men.   Pure joy, real gladness, has no birthplace but that on this earth.   Those who seek to serve God, to please God, and to despise the world, feel a joy very different from the poisoned joys of worldlings. Their joy is joy grounded on religion, altogether spiritual, all conformable with the nature of the soul; and this alone is able to content and satiate it. Their joy is a sweet joy, a tranquil joy, an abundant joy, which nothing can disturb, which must be possessed in order to form a right idea of it. There have been saints, and many of them, who have amorously complained of the excess of sweetness with which

their heart was inundated, of the abundance of their joy, and of the happiness with which their heart was filled.   Was there ever found one among the happy people of the world, of the great ones of the world, who has had to act thus?   Will there be found any to make complaints like these? What hinders you from tasting this genuine gladness?   What prevents your experiencing what the saints have experienced?   Do you yourself also become a saint; set your·self to love God, to serve God, to please God, and you will know by experience what sort of joy is felt in that state.

Fruit.—It is never a reasonable thing to take poison, under the pretext that it is pleasant to the taste, or with the intention to take antidotes with it. Consider all the joys of the world as mortal poisons.   Be on your guard against worldly feasts, against worldly joys, even the most lawful.   Join yourself to good people in their practices of piety, in their spiritual exercises, in visiting churches; but keep from profane amusements, where there breathes nothing but profligacy and licentiousness. Fly from noise and dissipation; love solitude and retirement; for there God speaks to the heart, and gives real gladness.

MAXIM XXVIII.

True happiness on earth consists in loving and serving God.

Reflections.

1. It is now a long time that people have been in search after happiness upon earth, but in vain; because happiness, even in this life, is not a produce of the earth. The world, though magnificent in its promises, has, till now, never been able to make any but unhappy people. Even in the midst of abundance, in the most flourishing prosperity, under the fairest smiles of fortune, people must confess that they are not happy, and that all this is not

sufficient to make them happy. We have been created to love and serve God. God is our last end. God alone can make us happy. Let the slaves of the world talk as loud as they please, let them boast of a happiness which they do not possess, it will still remain true that happiness cannot be found, except in serving and loving our true and only happiness, which is God. Every other idea of happiness which people may form to themselves, is false and chimerical. Whoever seeks happiness otherwise than in serving God, is under illusion and in error; he will always be unhappy. People go on saying that the service of God is a heavy yoke; but Jesus Christ, who is the infallible truth, says that it is sweet. Can it be said that the yoke of the world is light or sweet? O ye children of the world, you are a set of slaves, victims of the tyranny of the world—a hard, barbarous, ungrateful master. Your condition is a piteous one; and yet you would make us believe that you are happy. Your heart gives the lie to your tongue. If in the service of God all those tortures, violences, vexations, displeasures, bitternesses, had to be endured, which must be endured in serving the world, I know not how many servants God would find; not many. But after all, have we been created to serve the world, to make the world our idol? Is this cruel tyrant our last end? No. Therefore a man cannot be happy in serving the world, since by doing so he departs from his happiness, which consists in loving and possessing his last end. Do you wish to be happy? Serve God, serve him with fidelity, love him with sincerity, obey him with punctuality, follow his laws; in this obedience, in this love, you will find happiness the most sweet and most charming.

2. In order to be happy it is necessary that the heart be at ease, be contented; that peace should rule in it. It is to no purpose that a man be powerful and rich. In vain he floats amidst pleasures and delights. He

will never be happy if his heart is not contented; peace in the soul can alone constitute his happiness. Now, God alone can content the heart of man. Whatever there is besides God may distract him, may charm him for a moment, may even give him a little joy; but as to fully contenting him, keeping him in peace, this is not possible; and that we say with certainty. Six thousand years and more have been demonstrating this truth, by faith, by reason, and by experience, and yet people will not believe. Why do you wonder that the world is full of unhappy people? The heart was made for God. If it does not love God, if it does not serve God, its love and its service is divided among a hundred masters, who agree in nothing among themselves except in imposing most hard laws, exacting painful sacrifices and servile submission, forbidding their slaves even to complain of their misery. Such is the disgraceful bondage under which the lovers of the world live in it—never one bright day, never one tranquil night, never one moment of peace; and can the heart be contented in a condition so tormenting, far from God, who is the only source of real satisfaction and real happiness. But, on the other hand, how great is the satisfaction of a heart which serves God! What a delight not to depend any longer on so many masters, to have no one to please but God only! The servant of God is happy, even in adversities; and in the midst of the greatest misfortunes, faith strengthens him, hope sustains him, charity consoles and animates him, interior grace mitigates his pains, the sight of heaven comforts him and fills him with the most exquisite sweetness. And is not this being happy? Is not this true felicity? People seek, study, belabour themselves to find barely the shadow of another happiness upon earth; but not one can ever say, I am happy, save inasmuch as he loves and serves God.

3. In order to be happy all our desires must be satisfied; and there is no

created good which does not whet the
appetite it is intended to satiate. The
passions are the tyrants of our hearts;
an abundance of created goods only
stimulates them, provokes them, and
makes them more insatiable than ever.
The very fountain at which the worldling intends to slake the thirst of his
desires, is found to be a spring of new
inclinations and new dissatisfactions.
The multiplicity of pleasures, is a
multiplicity, ever increasing, of dis-
gusts and afflictions. Honours, titles,
greatness give a kind of pleasure, but
they are all kneaded with bitterness,
since they never succeed in satisfying
the desires of the heart. Our heart is
made for an infinite good, and no other
good can satisfy it than God, the fountain of all good. In nothing, therefore,
save in God, can man find his happiness. In the service of God, the passions are put in chains, the conscience
is in peace, the desires are quieted,
because nothing is desired except the
pleasing of him, and that can be always at hand. Where is the worldling

content with the master he serves? How many complaints, of not being sufficiently recompensed, of being over-burthened, of not giving satisfaction! On the other hand, there is not a single saint who is not content, who is not overwhelmed with joy in God's service. Was there one ever yet found who could complain of God not being a good and kind master? Or that he had not the secret of satisfying the desires of the heart? Can eighty years, passed in the service of the world, give as much tranquillity or consolation at the hour of death, as a few days spent in loving and serving God? How many great ones and happy ones of this world, would wish to enjoy peace of heart at that great moment! How long, O my God, shall I be so hostile to my own interests, that seeing I may be happy in loving and serving thee, I keep myself miserable and unhappy by serving the world? Let him who wishes take the world for a master; thou, O God, wilt alone be mine.

Fruit.—Your happiness depends, sc to speak, upon yourself, since it depends from yourself to be what you ought to be. Know that, only in serving God can you be happy. Make it a rule to yourself to serve God with fervour, and you will soon serve him with pleasure. Resolve to obey him in all things, to follow him, to listen to him, let the world say what it will, and you cannot but be happy. Love and practise interior recollection; without that, piety and devotion soon languish. Mortify your curiosity with regard to things of the world, and say to all its inducements: *God is my master; him will I serve.*

MAXIM XXIX.

God should not be loved by halves.

Reflections.

1. God is not content with half-love. Loving God by halves means having a weak will—a half-will of

M

loving him. It is, at the most, wishing to obey him in what he prescribes under pain of damnation, but caring very little about the rest. Not loving God, except by halves, is a wishing to please him in certain points, with a disposition to displease him; and, in point of fact, displeasing him in others. It is a love that pretends to be for God, but is, in reality, for the world—for ourselves, in preference to everything, since it is a following of our own inclinations. Can God be pleased with this division? Nothing gives God greater dishonour, if I may so speak, than a divided heart. How can God approve of it? To know God, to know what he wills, and yet to deny him; to know what displeases him, and then to displease him—what kind of insult can be more injurious to him than this? Can he be pleased with such conduct? This is an imitation of the devils, who know him and fear him, but, wretches that they are, never love him. What has been your love of God up to this? To love God by halves, is not loving.

2. To divide the heart between God and creatures, is unjust. God alone has made our heart. He alone has purchased it at the cost of the precious blood of his Son. Our heart ought, therefore, to be his entirely. God does not ask the half of our heart; he requires it all, and he cannot demand less. Not to give it to him entirely, is the same as not to give it at all. Can there be a greater injustice! Our heart is such a paltry thing; perhaps it will be too much, then, to give it all to God? God, perchance, cannot fill it, and so we ought to look for creatures wherewith to gratify it? Nothing can certainly be more injurious to the majesty of God than this division of love—nothing more unjust, after he has commanded us to love him with all our heart. But, perhaps, God is not enough for you, and you must go and beg for something else. And where, pray, will you find your happiness, if not in God? God will

be for ever the perfect felicity of the saints in heaven, and he cannot be yours here on earth. Oh! how wretched is the being for whom God is not sufficient!

3. The division of the heart between God and the world is impossible. We cannot serve two masters, our Saviour says, especially when the masters are so opposed as are the world and Jesus Christ. Their laws, their tendencies, their maxims, their interests, are too diverse to be capable of coalition. A person cannot love one without hating the other, and to wish to please one and other is to displease both. Search out all the expedients you please, observe all possible circumspection, the spirit of the world will extinguish the spirit of Jesus Christ. If you wish to serve and love the world, God will chase you from his service; God will refuse your love. If you wish to please the world, you immediately displease God. What impiety! what madness! to imagine you can possibly please both! Do you want to make

a compromise which no one has ever yet been able to bring about—nay, which our Lord himself has condemned? What agreement, says St. Paul, can there be between light and darkness? between Christ and Belial? You have but one master, and that is God; but one heart, and that must be wholly his. Love therefore and serve God alone. How long is it that you have denied God the perfect sacrifice of your heart by sharing it with creatures? Make up this very day for this injury you have done your God.

Fruit.—If you do not love God with your whole soul, with your whole heart, with your whole strength, you do not love in very deed. Take away from your heart, and cut off at once any affection which is not for God or in order to God. Determine every morning upon the proofs of your love you intend giving him during the day: for example, of not getting angry, of not becoming impatient, of giving up this pleasing conversation, of performing that practice of devotion, of overcoming that natural failing; in a word, of never doing or omitting anything whereby God might be displeased.

MAXIM XXX.

God rewards with great munificence those who serve him.

Reflections.

1. To serve God is the most essential duty of man, and it ought to be reward enough for man to have the honour of being allowed to serve him. Nevertheless, God wishes that our services may be our merits, and he gives an infinite recompense to the smallest proof of our obedience. Consider a moment what goodness, what care, what liberality God shows towards those who love him sincerely and serve him faithfully. Without speaking of the temporal blessings, of the evident prosperity, that is often to be seen in the house of the just man; let us but count up the number of salutary inspirations, of special aids, the flood of

graces, the reward of merits, and the price of the blood of Jesus Christ, so many supernatural gifts more valuable than all the world can contain, which are often given in return for some small act of charity, one little act of the love of God, a bare desire of a just soul. It might be said that God forgets these infinite goods he gives us, from the moment we cause him, so to say, to repeat them by our fidelity to grace. When there is question of recognising and rewarding our little services, God consults only his own divine heart. The most exquisite peace of conscience, far excelling all the pleasures of sense, an interior fund of consolation, preferable to all profane joys, are the usual return God gives for the very least acts of virtue. With a kindness which is tenderness itself, does God animate and encourage his least servants. *Well done, faithful servant, I will place thee over many things; I will give thee much to rule.* What consolation is this! And with what solidity and sweetness is it not fraught!

Oh! what a good master God is!   But, alas! are we not void of common sense, aye, of faith, if we have need of so many arguments to persuade us that we ought to serve such a Lord?

2. If God did nothing else but be pleased at our services, we should be highly recompensed indeed; but his munificent heart will not be content with this.   God works even miracles to recompense those who serve him; and he takes a particular pleasure in providing for their necessities after a manner that will make them feel the sweetness of his protection.   It might be said that God is occupied only in caring for his servants.   We are travellers in this world, and we walk difficult ways; what does not God do daily to prevent his servants from deviating from or failing in the proper path?   His angels are employed about them, his graces are directing them, he himself guides and advises them by secret inspirations as to what they are to do, and what to avoid.   How many miracles has not God performed, and

how many does he not perform every day for his own faithful servants! He makes the waves solid under the feet of a St. Francis of Paula; he feeds St. Paul in the desert by means of a raven; he preserves St. John unhurt in a cauldron of boiling oil. Let all the earth be armed, let hell itself be let loose against the servants of God; what have they to fear under the protection of their Lord? With what zeal, with what particular concern does not God protect them! He holds them in his hands, nay, carries them in his heart; he has the very hairs of their heads numbered, and declares that he will so guard them as that all men cannot pluck one single hair off them. Good God! how loving is thy goodness; how touchingly bountiful is it towards those who serve thee! Yet, strange to say, though God is so kind, so good towards those who serve him, so few are to be found who serve him with gladness and perseverance, whilst the world, which is universally acknowledged to be an inhuman, cruel,

and ungrateful master, finds crowds
who serve it like slaves.   In vain does
it treat them tyrannically, pay them
back with tears, and give them sorrow
for their wages; still we scarcely find
one who does not serve it with delight,
and rejoice in his unhappy lot.   Let
the world be unjust, let it be even
cruel, its service will only advance,
and every day will make an addition
to the ranks of its slaves.   God, on the
contrary, heaps benefits on his servants;
he rewards even the good will.
Although nothing be done for him, he
pays liberally the very desire of doing
good; nothing escapes, everything is
remunerated, everything is rewarded
in his service: and God is badly
served!   Scarcely can one be found
who wishes to serve him!   Alas! some
are ashamed of being reputed his servants.   What a fearful contradiction
between faith and actions is this!
Declare yourself to-day willing to
serve God, and be ashamed only of
serving him negligently.

3. Consider the recompense God has

prepared for his servants in the next life; cast your eyes for a moment upon the precious crown, upon the immensity of the eternal blessings with which God is pleased to repay your services in heaven, and then say his liberality is not boundless. He does not wish to make mention, on the great day of retribution, save of what is done by his servants, ordinarily, noiselessly, and easily. For a glass of water, for a little coin, given for his sake, for a tear shed over the miseries of others, for a visit paid to poor invalids, he gives a torrent of delights, an eternal felicity, an ocean of consolation, the joys of the Lord, a paradise of content, and, as if this were too little, and not at all sufficient, he himself will he give as the recompense of his servants. Come, you blessed of my Father, our Saviour will say, possess the kingdom which has been prepared for you. This kingdom is yours; you have merited it, you have purchased it. And with what? And how? With a little violence you have offered to your senses, with a little victory over your passions, with a little mortification, with the brief retirement of a few days. What proportion, O God, is there between the reward and the service, the recompense and the labour? The kingdom of heaven, eternal happiness, the beatitude of God himself is given for nothing!   Can there be difficulty in serving God?   Can it be believed that it costs too much to serve him?   This God, who does not forget even one step made for his love, a bare external act of reverence, and the least interior motion of which he is the object; but gives in return an eternal recompense!   O Lord, and is it possible thou hast so few servants?   Is it possible one can loathe thy service? Is it possible I can serve thee with disgust, with negligence? But have I any faith?   Do I know my religion? And why, then, do I not serve thee, my God, who deservest all my service—all my love?   This moment I dedicate myself entirely to thee, I will serve thee without reserve, I will serve thee for ever.

Fruit.—Consider to-day attentively what God requires of thee for so long a time, and what thou hast refused to give him of his demands: that little sacrifice—that short victory—that act of mortification—that modest reserve —that attention to your duties. If the world had asked them, it would have cost you nothing to give them. God has been asking them for many years, and do you still deny them? When will you yield? If to-day you declare yourself willing to serve God, to-day put an end to your dilatoriness, to-day resolve to do all that God requires of you. Do not get afraid at the difficulties of serving God; and when you perceive your courage slackening, remember that God himself will be the recompense of all you do. Will not your hardest sacrifice be amply rewarded by this? Keep this maxim always before your mind.

MAXIM XXXI.

True devotion to the Blessed Virgin is a source of grace, and a sign of predestination.

Reflections.

1. The choicest favours of heaven are reserved to the clients of Mary, since they are all trusted to her hands or laid up in her heart, she being appointed the gracious dispenser of them. All servants of God partake of them, for she is mother of all; but her clients, those who love her, are preferred to others, are singled out by Mary, and in Mary they find every help, every succour, every grace, every comfort. We live in a hostile country: how many temptations, how many dangers, how many plots are laid for our innocence! Our life is a continual warfare: our weakness makes us tremble; the frequent occasions of falling put our salvation in jeopardy. We want very powerful graces, and without a potent protection who can promise himself to come

off victorious? A true client of Mary
has all great remedies at hand. He
serves a queen who has power, without restriction, over all hell; he is
the son of a mother who has a most
tender heart, and has in her hand all
the treasures of grace; he loves a lady
whose bounty is equal to her power.
Oh, what place of safety can be more
secure than that of her protection!
True devotion to Mary assures us of
every succour. If Mary protects us,
we have nothing to fear in this place
of exile. If the Mother of Mercy defend us, no enemy can hurt us. And
if Mary is so liberal towards those
who are indifferent and cold about
her, what must be her bounty towards
her faithful servants—towards her
own dear favourites! All kinds of
good things, says St. Antoninus, have
come to me from the hands of Mary.
Have you the happiness of being of
the number of the servants of Mary,
and of her clients? You have found
your destiny, you have found the
fountain of graces, and the mine of

every good. Are you in favour with Mary? Are you dedicated to her service? You have found those arms against hell, which God puts into the hands of those whom he wishes to be saved. You are in a place of safety; take care not to go out therefrom, nor deserve to lose the love of so great a queen.

2. Mary not only defends her clients against the temptations of hell, but consoles them in their sadness. She assists them in their necessities, she sustains them in their conflicts, she consoles them in their afflictions. The title of Mother of Mercy, which Mary carries engraven on her heart, expresses all this. We shall never know sufficiently the treasures of grace, the unspeakable advantages which are found in this devotion, which was always so dear to the saints, who could never find terms sufficient to express the sentiments of love, confidence, veneration, and tenderness, they had for this most loving of mothers. But the most singular benefit

this devotion procures us, is the assistance of Mary at the hour of our death. There is no moment more important, no moment more terrible, no moment of such serious consequence, as that of our death. In this most important moment, the servants of Mary find an all-powerful protection in her. And as this point is decisive of our salvation, this loving mother is never more solicitous, never more generous towards those who have loved and honoured her, than when it comes. And who can more reasonably or more securely promise themselves this propitious assistance, than the true servants of Mary? Will she forget, in the hour of need, those who have loved her during their life? What a consolation in our last illness, to think we shall die clients of Mary! What may not one expect from the Sovereign Judge, when the Judge's mother is advocate? A well-founded confidence in the bounty of Mary at this last moment, sweetens all its pains, and tempers all its horrors. There are very few clients of Mary, who do not die with this sweet and religious tranquillity, and almost certain presage of their eternal happiness. Would *you* like to die thus? Dedicate yourself to-day as a faithful servant, a devout client of Mary's, for ever.

3. The most reasonable desire, and the most consoling hope, is that of being among the number of the elect. All the goods of this world cannot satisfy the heart, for eternity shakes its dread over them. One may be content about what actually is, but one has reason always to fear what is to be. Shall I be among the number of the predestined? Shall I be saved? Shall I be condemned? This is the uncertainty that terrifies one. Oh! how happy should we be, if we could have but some sure presage of our eternal happiness! Here is an almost certain sign: have a true, tender, and constant devotion to Mary, and you have a sure sign of your salvation. Devotion to Mary is a particular grace which God bestows upon those

whom he has destined by his mercy for glory, by inspiring them with love and confidence for her who is to obtain for them the grace to merit it. All the saints agree in putting this devotion down as a character of the predestinate. All the grace of salvation, all the hope of life, says St. Thomas of Villanova, is in Mary. It is not possible, says St. Germain, that a true client of Mary should perish. And who can imagine that this mother of charity would let any of those children be lost, whom Jesus consigned to her on Calvary? Who can think for a moment that this tender mother could bear to see lost eternally those children which cost herself so much pain, and Jesus all his blood? No, it is not possible. Wherefore, to be a child of Mary, to love and be devout to this divine mother, is a sign of predestination. Hence, no one has ever seen a Christian who has persevered in this devotion, and has not died the death of the predestined. On the other hand, to be an enemy of devotion to Mary, to make little of her praises, to lessen her worship, to undervalue demonstrations of reverence towards her, to have an irreligious coldness, a culpable indifference towards this queen of saints, this mother of mercy, is a certain mark of reprobation. Do you wish to make sure of your eternal salvation? Promise to-day, before heaven and earth, that you will be a faithful servant and a child of Mary.

Fruit.—Never be afraid of doing too much when there is question of showing your love and affection for Mary. Consider it an honour to be a servant of Mary, to celebrate her praises, to gain her a client, to be a member of some confraternity in which devotion to Mary is encouraged, promoted, and cherished. The devotion of her Rosary is one of the most solid you can practise; it is enriched also by the Church with many indulgences. Resolve to recite it every day. Every morning dedicate yourself as servant and child of Mary, place yourself under her protection, and offer her your heart often during the day. Take up the holy custom of showing her marks of reverence, saluting her images and visiting her chapels. Make, for love of her, some small sacrifice, such as, not looking at nor listening to some matter of curiosity, avoiding certain company; depriving yourself of some savoury morsel or lawful diversion. Let her vigils be for you days of greater abstinence and mortification than usual. Let her feasts be days of greater retirement, prayer, and recollection. Never omit, on those days, as far as you possibly can, to go to confession and communion.

END OF THE FIRST PART.

PART SECOND.

MORNING PRAYER.

Morning prayer is a duty which pleases God particularly, as being the first-fruits of the day. You ought, therefore, to offer it with pious affection. From the fidelity with which this duty is performed, depends the good success of the actions of the day ; and you shall have commenced them badly if you begin without having offered God your heart, asked him for the help of his grace, or thanked him for his gifts bestowed on you. Never deny our Lord this just tribute, and consequently, as soon as ever you get up in the morning, throw yourself upon the floor in the presence of God, and devoutly recite the following

PRAYER.

My God, I adore thee with sentiments of the most profound humility, and I render thee, with all my heart, the homage that is due to thy sovereign majesty. I thank thee most humbly for all the graces thou hast bestowed on me up to this moment. It is due to thy goodness alone that I live this day. I wish to employ it solely in serving and loving thee. I consecrate to thee all my thoughts, words, actions, and sufferings this day. Bless them, thou, O Lord, that they may be all animated by thy love, may all tend to thy glory, and the salvation of my soul.

My God, thou knowest my weakness, and how I can do nothing without the assistance of thy grace: do not deny it to me, O Lord, and grant it to me in proportion to my wants. Give me strength to avoid all the evil thou hast forbidden me, to practise all the good thou wishest from me, and to suffer patiently all the troubles thou shalt be pleased to send me. Grant that I may begin to-day to correct my vices, to fly sin, to detach my heart from all the false goods of this world; not to believe save in thee, not to hope save in thy promises, not to live save in thy love. Fortify my heart against all temptations, and grant that I may always walk in thy divine presence, and in the way of thy holy commandments.

Adorable Jesus, divine model of Christian perfection, I wish to apply myself to-day, as much as possible, to making myself like to thee—sweet, humble, chaste, patient, charitable—and I shall make, with thy grace, all possible efforts not to fall to-day into the sins I have so often committed, and by which I have so often displeased thy divine heart.

[Here resolve to avoid that particular sin to which you are habitually prone. Forecast occasions in order to shun them. Renew your resolutions over and over, and ask for more grace.]

An Act of Faith.

I firmly believe, because God, the infallible truth, has so revealed it to the holy Catholic Church, and through her also to me, that there is One God in Three divine Persons, equal and distinct, which are called the Father, the Son, and the Holy Ghost; that the Son became man, taking, by the operation of the Holy Ghost, flesh and a human soul in the womb of the most pure Virgin Mary; that he died for us on the cross, arose again, ascended into heaven, and thence shall come, at the end of the world, to judge all the living and the dead, to give to the righteous paradise, and to the wicked hell for ever. And, moreover, through the same motive, I believe all those things which the same holy Church believes and teaches.

An Act of Hope.

My God, because thou art omnipotent, and infinitely good and merciful, I hope that, through the merits of the passion and death of Jesus Christ our Saviour, thou wilt give me eternal life, which thou hast faithfully promised to whomsoever does the works of a good Christian, works which I am resolved to do with thy assistance.

An Act of Charity.

My God, because thou art the supreme and most perfect good, I love thee with my whole heart, and above all things; and, rather than offend thee, I am disposed to lose all beside; and for love of thee, I wish to love my neighbour as myself.

An Act of Contrition.

My God, since thou art the supreme goodness, and since I love thee above all things, I am sorry, and grieve from my heart for having offended thee; and purpose firmly, with the help of thy grace, never to sin for the time to come, and especially to avoid the proximate occasions of sin.

DEDICATION OF ONESELF TO THE BLESSED VIRGIN.

. Most holy Mary, Virgin Mother of God, I, *N. N.*, although most unworthy of being thy servant, yet, moved by thy wonderful tenderness of maternal affection for me, and the desire to serve thee, choose thee this day, in presence of thy divine Son, of my guardian angel, and all the heavenly court, for my special mistress, advocate, and mother; and firmly resolve, with thy aid, to serve thee henceforth, and do my best to get others to serve thee also. I humbly beseech thee, O kindest of mothers, through the precious blood of thy Son, that you receive me among thy devout clients as your perpetual servant; favour me in my actions, and obtain for me the grace so to deport myself in all my thoughts, words, and actions, that I may never offend thy Son Jesus. Remember me, and do not abandon me, now, nor at the hour of my death. Amen.

NIGHT PRAYERS.

IF it be important to begin the day well, it is no less so to conclude it in like manner. The new graces which God has given you in the course of the day, and the protection you need in order to pass the night without danger, are so many reasons why you should have recourse to our Lord, and consecrate the last moments of the day to him. On your knees, then, before the majesty of God, before undressing, say the following

PRAYER.

I adore thee, my God, with all the respect which the presence of thy sovereign greatness infuses into me. I humble myself before thee, who art my Creator, my last end, my all, my absolute Lord.

I thank thee, O Lord, for all the favours thy mercy has been pleased to grant me. Thou hast loved me from eternity, thou hast drawn me from nothing. Thou hast given thy life to redeem me, thou hast showered on me a multitude of favours every day. Ah! Lord, what can I do in return for so much? Ye angels and saints of hea- ven, praise and thank for me the God of mercies, who does not cease to bestow favours on the most unworthy and ungrateful of his creatures.

My God, I know that I have to die; and perhaps shall never rise from the bed on which I am about to lie. At the hour of my death, O Lord, I shall wish to have never offended thee, and to have always loved thee; put me now into these holy dispositions. Yes, O my God, I detest all my sins for love of thee; I am sorry for them from my heart, because they displease thee. Behold me, O God, at thy feet, covered with confusion, and pierced with grief at the sight of my sins. I humbly ask pardon, and conjure thee, by the merits of Jesus Christ, to give me the grace never more to offend thee, never more to displease thee, always to love thee. Yes, this minute, I renounce sin and its occasions, and I intend, with thy assistance, to avoid it with all my power, to be faithful and obedient to thy holy law, to live and die in thy holy love.

My God, I believe in thee because

thou art truth itself. I hope in thee, because thou art faithful to thy promises. I love thee, O my God, with all my heart, because thou art infinitely amiable.

Bless, O my God, the repose I am about to take according to thy holy will. Defend me, during the night, from the snares of the infernal enemy; guard me, protect me, and save me from eternal death. My God, into thy hands I commend my soul.

O Mary, my mother, and the mother of God, I confirm and ratify, with all my heart, at thy feet, the entire consecration of myself already made to you. I choose you again for my protectress and mother, and I put myself under thy special protection. Assist me every instant of my life to my last breath, and do not abandon me till you see me safe in heaven.

My guardian angel, my patron saints, intercede for me. *Our Father, Hail Mary*, and *Glory be to the Father*, three times, in honour of the Passion, and three *Aves* to the Blessed Virgin.

PRAYERS FOR CONFESSION.

THERE is nothing of greater importance in the way of salvation, than the receiving the sacrament of penance with the necessary dispositions. One confession, well made, may be enough to make you a saint. Yet, after so many confessions, you are as you were before. Whence arises this? From your negligence in disposing yourself properly, and from not bringing to this sacrament the dispositions it requires. In order, therefore, that you may not find your death where you ought to have found life, endeavour to come always to confession with the necessary dispositions.

The most essential of these is sorrow. The priest can sometimes supply the defect of the examen by timely questions; but he can never supply sorrow when you have got none in your heart. Hence, if you wish to make a good confession, excite yourself with great care and zeal to a true sorrow for your sins, and do not be afraid of spending too much time in doing so. Without this interior, sincere, and supernatural sorrow, tears and sighs are good for nothing. Excite yourself, therefore, before confession, in frequent acts of contrition, and let them proceed from a penitent and humble heart. From this all the fruit of the sacrament depends. And since contrition is a gift of God, it must be asked of him with humility and fervour, begging of him also, at the same time, to give the dispositions for worthily receiving the sacrament of penance.

A prayer to beg of God the Dispositions for the Sacrament of Penance.

God of mercy, who art always ready to receive the repentant sinner and grant him pardon, cast a look of pity on a soul which once fled from thee, and now returns trying to wash off its stains in the salutary waters of penance. Give me the grace, O God, to come to this sacrament with the proper dispositions. Be thou in my spirit, that thy truth may make me know all my sins. Be thou in my heart, that thy love may make me detest them. Be thou in my mouth, that I may confess all with sincerity, and obtain full pardon for them: through the merits of Jesus Christ my Saviour.

A Prayer before Examination of Conscience.

Holy Spirit, source of truth, deign to communicate to me a ray of thy divine light, so that nothing may escape the close scrutiny I am about to make in my own interior of my evil deeds. Thou, who knowest the depths of my heart, show me its malice; let me know all my bad thoughts, even the most hidden; all my irregular desires, all my sinful actions, all the omissions of my duties, and the scandals I have occasioned to my neighbour. Enlighten me, O God of truth, and do not allow self-love to seduce or blind me; remove the veil which it has put before my eyes, so that nothing may hinder me from making myself known, as far as need be, to your minister. I desire to know my sins, only in order to weep for them before thee, to detest them, and to correct myself for the future.

Prayer to obtain true sorrow for sin.

Ah! my God, how can I after having loved sin so much and so long, conceive a sincere sorrow, a sore displeasure for it, if thou dost not infuse these sentiments into my soul by thy grace, if thou dost not give me true sorrow for having offended thee, and an efficacious resolution never to offend thee more?   Break the hardness of my heart, and draw therefrom tears of compunction, thou who alone canst change the rock of the desert into a fountain of living water.   Mingle the tears I shall shed in thy presence, with the tears and blood thy Son has shed for me, in order that they may become a salutary bath to give life and health to my soul.   My God, give me thy love, and for the sake of thy love, true sorrow for my sins.   This is the grace which I ask of thee, and which I sue for in the name of thy Divine Son, through the intercession of the Blessed Virgin, of my angel guardian and holy patrons.   Amen.

An Act of Contrition.

My Lord Jesus Christ, I confess and believe with a lively faith that thou art my God, infinitely good, infinitely amiable and merciful towards sinners. I hope and trust in thy infinite goodness, and I love thee above all things. I am sorry and grieve with all my heart for having offended thee. I am troubled, above all, at having displeased thee, my God, who art so infinitely good. I detest, I hate, and abominate all my sins, not only because by sinning I have lost heaven and deserved hell, but, much more, because I have lost thy grace, because I have offended thee, my most loving Father, my most amiable Lord, my God, my sovereign good, worthy of infinite love. Oh! if my sorrow could equal the heinousness of my offences! O Saviour, agonizing for me in the garden of Olives, pour into my heart one drop from that sea of bitterness which then flooded thy soul, and grant that I may be so sorry for my sins as to be ready to die. Yes, I am ready to make reparation for the offences I have committed, at the cost of anything most dear to me, yea, even life itself. Let it never happen, dear Jesus, that I should return again to sin, and displease thy most loving heart. I firmly purpose, by the help of thy grace, never more to offend thee, and to avoid every proximate occasion of sin.   I resolve and protest that for thy love I am determined to live in the state of grace, with thy assistance, until death.

An Act of Resolution.

Can it be, O Lord, that because thou art infinitely good to me, I should go on abusing thy mercy, to offend thee with impunity?   Ah! let it not be so for the time to come, O my God, thou who seest my most secret thoughts, knowest also the dispositions in which I now am, never to offend thee, to leave sin at any cost, to fly the occasions of sin, and labour resolutely at eradicating my evil habits.   I am determined, O Lord, and here renew my resolution at thy feet—*never more to sin.*   I shall engrave thy holy law upon the bottom of my heart, and I shall lose my life rather than fall away from the resolution I have formed of never offending thee, and always serving thee faithfully. The world will try to involve me in my former disorders; my passions will rise up against me, it will cost me a great deal to repress them; but with thy grace, O my God, I shall keep my word I plighted, in spite of the persecution of libertines and the repugnance of nature. "*I have sworn and resolved to keep the judgments of thy justice.*" Never again thoughts, words, or deeds against thy holy law; never more sins for me. Rather shall I die, rather shall I drop down dead before thee, than ever again offend thee by accursed sin. I hope for all this from thy grace, through the merits of Jesus Christ my Redeemer.

Prayer to be said immediately before Confession.

Be thou, my God, in my heart and on my lips, that I may make a sincere and complete confession of all my sins. Be thou also in the heart of thy minister to whom I go to present myself, in order that, filled with thy Spirit, which is a spirit of light, of wisdom, and of charity, he may be able to lay bare the depth of my wounds, and pour in the blood of thy Son to heal them; to teach me the term to which thou wouldst be pleased to conduct me, and the way by which I am to travel in order to reach thee safely and securely. I intend to offer this confession I am about to make for the glory of thy justice, to please thee by fulfilling thy holy will, and to procure thee the greatest honour I possibly can.

O Mary, my dear mother, you who are so tenderly inclined towards poor sinners, who have a sincere desire of being converted, assist me by your help, since you are, after God, my most dear hope, and obtain for me the grace to make this confession profitably. My guardian angel, come to my help. My holy patrons, pray for me, and obtain for me pardon for my sins through the merits of Jesus Christ.

Prayer to be said after Confession.

Shall I dare then to persuade myself, O my God, that I, from the sinner I was a while ago, am now, by the
grace of the sacrament, justified and
cleansed thoroughly from my sins?
Yes, O God of goodness, I have received holy absolution, and this merciful sentence has given me back thy
grace and restored me to thy friendship. This is the effect of the precious
blood which thou hast shed for me, O
amiable Redeemer; this is the fruit of
thy adorable wounds, whose power has
cured mine. To these do I owe my
reconciliation, my salvation. May thy
holy name be for ever blessed!—thy
mercy eternally praised. Ah! Lord,
what goodness has been thine, to be
contented with a light satisfaction instead of the eternal pains of hell, to
which I was justly condemned; to
pardon me all, to forget all, to take me
into thy bosom, and press me to thy
heart! God of mercy, God of goodness, what thanks can I render thee

sufficient to attest my sense of gratitude? But what can I do, O Redeemer of my soul, I, so miserable a creature? I shall exalt thy infinite mercy at least, and exalt it till my last breath. I shall glorify, during my whole life, a God so good, the best of masters, the most sweet and loving of fathers: "*Exaltabo te, Deus meus Rex.*" In the meantime, I beseech thee, by the intercession of the Blessed Virgin, to defend me from all temptations, and give me the grace to overcome them, so that I may be able to keep inviolate until death the resolution I have made, and now confirm, from my heart, of dying rather than ever offend thee, since thou art my most loving God.

PRAYERS FOR COMMUNION.

THERE is no means left us for our sanctification by the goodness of our Redeemer more efficacious, there is no practice of devotion more proper for a Christian, and more dear and acceptable to the heart of Jesus, than holy communion. He himself invites us to this divine table, in a manner the most pressing and the most loving, desiring ardently to be united to our souls. It is the desire of holy Church that her children should communicate often; if it were possible, even every time they assist at Mass. We need light, to know the divine will concerning us; strength, to labour incessantly for our sanctification; and grace, to resist the temptations of our enemies, to apply ourselves seriously to live in the spirit of Jesus Christ, and to imitate his virtues. Now all this we get through holy communion, especially when it is frequent. By receiving Jesus Christ in person, we receive light in our spirit, our nourishment in a special way, the proper life of our soul; and feeding on his body and blood, we become partakers of his virtues, and enter into an interior communication with him.

But what is more important is the communicating well, with fervour, with the proper dispositions. One single communion, well made, is capable of raising a soul to the highest perfection, whereas, on the contrary, a sacrilegious communion is the most fearful of crimes, and is always fraught with sad and terrible consequences to the soul. To communicate profitably one ought to be in the grace of God, to have no voluntary attachment to venial sin, to dispose his soul with fervent acts of faith, charity, confidence, humility, and a great desire of being united to Jesus Christ in the sacrament. To facilitate this proximate preparation for communion, I propose to subjoin here some acts of virtue to be made immediately before receiving. But since it is the heart that ought to speak to our Lord, do not be content with a superficial reading of the following prayers; accompany them with an interior feeling of the heart, endeavouring to stir up within yourself the affections of the will which are signified by the words. Do the same with the acts of thanksgiving after receiving.

Go often to confession and communion if you wish solidly to amend your life, and make sure of the affair of your salvation.

BEFORE COMMUNION.

An Act of Faith.

My Lord Jesus Christ, I believe with a firm and lively faith that thou art true God and true man; the only begotten of the Father; the Second Person of the most Holy Trinity; the Word incarnate by the Holy Ghost in the chaste womb of the Blessed Virgin, of whom thou art a true and only Son.

I believe with a firm and lively faith that thou, the very same, art body and blood, soul and divinity, in the most holy sacrament instituted by thee for a testimony to men of the immense love thou bearest them. I believe that, in receiving holy communion this morning, I received thyself truly and entirely, my Saviour, my Redeemer, my God, my all.

An Act of Hope.

I hope, O my God, in thy infinite power, and confide in thy immense goodness. To possess thee shortly within my soul, oh, how my expectations of receiving great graces from thee increase! I hope for pardon of my sins, which I detest anew, and at which I am extremely grieved, since they displease thee so much, my God, amiable above all things. I hope and trust, by the merits of thy most holy passion and death, to obtain an increase of thy grace, and all the aids necessary for loving thee and serving thee faithfully, as well as keeping me from ever offending thee. I hope to obtain holy perseverance in thy love, and the eternal salvation of my soul.

An Act of Charity.

I love thee with my whole heart, my most amiable Jesus; I love thee with all my soul and all my strength. I ask pardon for not having loved thee up to this as I ought; and I declare that I am determined to love thee always for the future. I love thee above all things, simply because thou art infinitely good, and supremely worthy of being loved.

I love thee with unalloyed love; I love thee more than any created thing—more than my own life. I wish I could love thee with an infinite love; and since thou givest me thyself entirely, I beg of thee to remove from my soul the least impediment to thy divine love, so that I can, with all the fulness of my heart, love thee in life, love thee in death, and love thee for all eternity.

An Act of Humility and Contrition.

Am I, then, a miserable creature, a vile worm, a most unworthy sinner, about to receive into my breast the Son of God, the King of glory, the Saint of saints? Ah! Lord, though I had the sanctity of all the angels and blessed of heaven, I would not yet be worthy to receive thee; how much the more unworthy must I feel, finding myself full of passions, of bad habits, of ingratitude and sins. More unworthy still for coming to receive thee without fervour, without preparation, without devotion, with such coldness, such indifference! Ah! my Jesus, I do not know what to do, except to humble myself in thy divine presence, to acknowledge my baseness, my vileness, and to implore thy infinite mercy. Thou well knowest how often, by most unpardonable acts of rebellion, I have driven from my heart thee, who art its true, its lawful, and only master, to make room for sin—for the devil.

Now I admit and confess my malice, my perfidy. I wish I had died a thousand times, rather than to have so basely offended thee. I ask pardon for having done so, with the deepest sorrow of my heart. I detest all my sins; I am sorry and grieve for them, since they have been offensive to a God so infinitely good. I will never offend thee again; I promise, with thy assistance, rather to die than be guilty of another offence against thee.

An Act of Oblation.

What can I do now to supply for my unworthiness? I offer thee, my Jesus, the sanctity, the love, and the fervour with which thy special and most chosen souls have received thee. I offer thee the immaculate heart of Mary, and those perfect and fervent acts with which she received thee so many times in the communion. I offer thee that ineffable sanctity with which thou receivedst thyself at the Last Supper, the only communion in which thou hast ever been received in a manner worthy of thyself.

I offer thee, through the hands of the Blessed Virgin, this communion I am about to make, to the honour and glory of the Blessed Trinity, in thanksgiving for the bitter passion and death thou hast endured for love of me. I offer it to thee in return, by way of a thanks, for all the graces and benefits thou hast ever bestowed upon me and upon the whole world. I offer it to thee, to obtain from thy goodness final perseverance, and the helps necessary to save me. I offer to thee for the conversion of poor sinners, for the salvation of my parents, friends, benefactors, and to obtain the pardon of all my own heavy sins. I offer it to thee for all the needs of holy Church, and for the wants of my own poor soul. Finally, I offer it to thee for the relief of the holy souls in purgatory, especially those who are most destitute, or have special claims upon my suffrages.

Prayer to the Blessed Virgin.

O most pure and immaculate Mother of my Jesus, this morning I am about to receive that same God who became incarnate in your virginal womb; and, oh! how loathsomely clothed with guilt is this soul I present as the receptacle of this God of purity! Most tender Mother, have pity on my misery! For the love of your Son, that he may be received, at least, less un- worthily, offer him for me the purity, the humility, the charity, and all the preparation you made when he became incarnate in your womb, and when you received him in this blessed sacra- ment.

My angel guardian, guide and con- duct me to the sacred table. Suggest to me acts of adoration, of humility, and of love, befitting so holy an action, and present them together with your own and those of your heavenly companions, who surround the sacred altar.

AFTER COMMUNION.

An Act of Adoration.

O Jesus, King of glory, and Lord of such supreme majesty, how hast thou ever deigned to come in person and visit a most vile worm of the earth, a miserable sinner such as I am?

I adore thee, my God, my Creator, my Redeemer, with the lowest abasement, the most profound reverence I am able. I desire that all should know thee, adore thee, and love thee.

I adore thee, most holy soul of my Jesus, here present; sanctify my soul with all its powers. I adore thee, most pure body of my Jesus; purify, by the contact of thy sacred flesh, my body and all its tendencies. I adore thee, ineffable divinity, united to the humanity of my Jesus, and I unite my adorations to all those which thou actually receivest in heaven from all the choirs of angels, from the Blessed Virgin and all the saints.

P

Act of Thanksgiving.

What shall I give thee, O my most sweet Jesus, in return for the great gift thou hast bestowed on me in giving me thyself? Let all the angels and saints in heaven bless thee and thank thee for me. I offer thee the thanks thy most holy Mother gave thee after her communion, and those which thou gavest to thy Father at the institution of this divine sacrament. I thank thee, my Jesus, as far as I know and am able to do so, for the infinite charity with which thou hast given me thyself. I thank thee for the ineffable benefit of coming to be the food of my soul. I wish I could have a thousand tongues and a thousand hearts to thank thee, to love thee. Fill up and perfect thy mercies in my regard; grant that I may derive that fruit from the favour done me this morning, which thou wishest me to draw. Grant that this communion may not serve to my greater damnation, but to the profit and salvation of my soul.

Act of Petition.

My God, can I doubt that thy goodness will grant me whatever I ask? Canst thou, who so liberally gavest thy very self, deny me thy gifts? I am unworthy, it is true, to get thy graces; but thou wilt glorify thy mercy in having compassion on me.

I ask from thee, therefore, the pardon of all my sins from the depths of my heart. I ask from thee, by the merits of thy passion, final perseverance in grace and in thy love, a holy death, and the saving of my soul. Give me courage and power to resist all the temptations of the devil, to conquer my passions, to mortify my evil inclinations, so that I may never fall into sin again. I ask from thee also all the temporal blessings which thou knowest to be most expedient for my eternal salvation.

I ask from thee, finally, my Jesus, thy blessing; give it to my soul, that it may be to me a pledge of the glory I hope from thy mercy, and which I implor-

ingly beg. through the merits of thy
precious blood.

Act of Oblation.

I offer thee, my Jesus, my liberty,
with all the powers of my soul. Take
my memory, and make it always call
thee to my mind. Take my intellect,
and grant me the blessing of always
thinking of thee. Take my will, and
make it one with thine own; let it love
only thee.

To thee I offer all the senses of my
body; grant me the grace that with
none of them may I ever displease thee
for the time to come.

I offer thee all my thoughts, words,
and actions, in union with the merits of
thy passion; in union with the merits
of the Blessed Virgin, and all the
saints; intending that all may be for
thy greater glory, and either a preparation or thanksgiving for thy holy
sacraments.

I offer thee my heart, with all its
affections; grant that I may never employ it otherwise than in loving thee,

my dear Redeemer. I hope I shall love thee in life, love thee in death, and throughout a blessed eternity.

Prayer to the Blessed Virgin.

Most holy Virgin, Mother of God, and my most loving mother, I come to offer thee my poor thanks, and implore the aid of thy protection. You can do all things with the Omnipotent, and your goodness and tenderness for men equals your power in heaven.

You know, O holy Virgin, how that from my infancy I have always looked upon you as my mother, my advocate, my special patron, and you have been pleased to regard me as one of your children. I confess, in the deep sense of my acknowledgment, that all the graces I have received from God came to me through you. Oh! that I was as faithful in loving and serving you, my dear mother, as you have been good in assisting me! But I will be so for the future: let the rest of my life be employed in honouring and loving you.

Receive, then, amiable mother, the declaration I make of being your perpetual client; accept the confidence I place in you; obtain for me from your dear Son, my Saviour, a lively faith, a firm hope, an ardent, generous, and constant charity. Obtain for me a purity of heart and body that nothing may ever stain—a patience and submission to the divine will which nothing can disturb.   Finally, my dear mother, Mary, obtain for me the grace to imitate you faithfully in the practice of all virtues during my life, that I may thereby deserve your assistance at the hour of my death, and the eternal happiness of the blessed in the kingdom of heaven.   Amen.

THE HOLY SACRIFICE OF THE MASS.

THE holy Mass is the sacrifice of the body and blood of Jesus Christ. It is the same sacrifice which he offered on Mount Calvary, renewed in an unbloody manner upon our altars. The Christian who is about to hear Mass ought to be convinced that there is no action which deserves to be performed with greater respect, devotion, and attention, than that of assisting at this august sacrifice. He ought to look upon the priest that celebrates as the person of Jesus Christ himself, who goes to lay down his life for the salvation of men, endeavouring to accompany him in this action of infinite love, with a spirit of immolation, interiorly offering himself to die and be sacrificed for him. He ought, in a word, to assist with the same respect, faith, devotion, and sorrow for his sins, he would have had did he see Jesus Christ crucified over again.

The way of assisting at Mass, which corresponds best with the nature of the sacrifice, and is most conformable to the intentions of our divine Lord, is that of thinking on the passion and death of our Redeemer, who, in instituting the blessed sacrament, wished that as often as those sacred mysteries should be celebrated, we would call to mind his sufferings : "This, as often as you shall do, do in remembrance of me."

There are many devout ways of hearing Mass to be found in different pious manuals. If you do not happen to have any of those at hand, you make use of the following, in which I have tried to assign to the different actions of the priest some devout thought on the passion, with a corresponding aspiration.

A METHOD OF ASSISTING DEVOUTLY AT MASS.

1. On your way to Mass, go as the Blessed Virgin did to Calvary, to assist at the death of her Son, and offer him in sacrifice to God for the salvation of men. Say to our Lord: I go, my sweet Jesus, to Calvary with thee; make me, I beseech thee, partaker of that charity which brought thee upon this painful mountain; give me the sentiments of grief and compassion which the daughters of Sion had when they saw thee led through the streets of Jerusalem, bound, crowned with thorns, and burthened with the wood of thy cross; give me that resignation to thy holy will which Mary, thy mother, had at the foot of the cross; and through the merits of thy pains,

and of her constancy, grant me perseverance in thy holy love.

2. Entering the church, raise up your spirit to God, and say, prostrate at the feet of the crucified: O infinite goodness of my God, what could ever have induced thee to suffer so much for me! I see none other than thy excessive love. O love of Jesus, I offer thee all my intentions, actions, and affections, ardently wishing that thou mayest be for ever the only love of my soul.

3. As Mass begins, collect your thoughts, and make the following aspirations: What return can I make to thee, O God, for the honour of allowing me to be present at so great a sacrifice? Jesus, my loving Redeemer, unite my heart to thee, and grant that my mind may not be otherwise engaged during the Mass, than in thinking of thee and on thy holy passion. Eternal Father, receive the sacrifice the priest is about to offer in satisfaction for my sins.

4. At the *Confiteor,* humble yourself

profoundly before the majesty of God, considering yourself as a culprit exceedingly guilty, coming to beg for mercy and forgiveness. Call to mind that Jesus Christ has taken your sins upon himself, and offered his life to satisfy for them. Ask of God, through the merits of the passion, pardon for all your faults. My Father and my God, I have sinned, I have offended thy sovereign goodness; ah! how the evil I have done displeases me above all things; but I beg of thee to forgive me, through the sufferings of thy Son.

5. At the *Gloria in excelsis Deo*, enter into the sentiments of the holy angels who entoned this joyful canticle for the first time, when they announced to the world the peace and reconciliation brought by Jesus Christ. Praise, adore, and bless God with the priest. Desire that his name may be known and glorified by all men, and that his kingdom be spread and propagated all over the earth. Be thou blessed for ever, O eternal Father, for having given thy only Son to be our Saviour.

Be thou praised and glorified for ever in thy infinite goodness, O Jesus, my Redeemer. I thank thy love which brought thee so many, such cruel torments, and so painful a death for me.

6. Whilst the priest reads the Epistle and Gospel, if you can understand him, listen with devout attention as to the words of God. If you do not understand him, or are too far away from the altar, beg of our Lord, with great fervour, that he would deign to enkindle the light of his holy faith in the hearts of all infidels, bring to the bosom of his Church all heretics, and convert by the efficacy of his grace all sinners. Ah! my God, enlighten all those unfortunate nations who know thee not. Diffuse throughout the world the light of thy Gospel. Dear Jesus, have pity on so many unhappy souls, who have cost thee thy precious blood, and lie in the darkness of infidelity and steeped in sin.

7. At the *Credo*, renew with humble submission the profession of your faith. My God, I believe all that

which the Church believes and proposes to me to be believed. Lord, I thank thee with all my heart, for the great blessing of the true faith which thou hast given me. In this faith I am resolved to live and die, and to give my life and blood, even in the midst of torments, for the confession thereof.

8. At the *Offertory*, place your heart, your soul, your body, your earthly goods, your hopes, your parents, your friends, and in general all your holy desires upon the sacred paten. Present all to God, that they may be immolated to him, together with the body of his divine Son, as a perfect holocaust in the order of sweetness. Beg of the divine Goodness to change you and transform you wholly into the Victim that is about to be sacrificed. Ah! thou art being sacrificed for me, and shall not I sacrifice myself entirely to thee? Why have I not a thousand hearts, a thousand bodies, a thousand lives, that I might sacrifice them all to thee, O Lord? Eternal Father, re-

ceive the sacrifice Jesus is offering, and permit me to be united to him.

9. At the *Lavabo*, desire to wash and purify your soul in the precious blood of Jesus Christ; beseech this divine Victim to give you a new heart entirely animated with his Spirit. Wash, O Lord, my soul in thy divine blood from all its uncleanness. Grant me a heart after thine own, and destroy in me all wrong and vicious affections. Renew my spirit, and sanctify it with thy grace.

10. At the *Preface*, raise up your heart to heaven, recollecting that Jesus has opened it for you at the cost of painful death. Renew the intention for which especially you offer the Mass, either for some spiritual necessity of yourself or your neighbour, or for some special grace. My God, by the infinite merits of the passion and death of Jesus Christ contained in this holy sacrifice, I beg of thee to grant me (*mention here what particular grace you wish for*). Yes, I ask them for the sake of the wounds of my suffering Redeemer.

11. After the *Sanctus*, keep yourself recollected in lively faith, considering the priest as personating Jesus Christ himself, the Mediator between God and men, who is treating on the great affair of your salvation. Go on devoutly meditating on the passion, resting on some particular point of it, such as the crucifixion, the agony, the ignominious and cruel death, which the Son of God has endured for you.

12. At the *Elevation* of the host, adore profoundly, with lively faith and abasement, your God there really present, bowing down at the same time moderately and respectfully. Look upon your Lord in the hands of the priest as on the arms of the cross, where he is sacrificed for you with excess of love. Offer Jesus Christ in the blessed sacrament to the divine Father as the victim of propitiation for your sins. Beg of him, through the merits of his Son, thus humbled, to have mercy on your soul. Dear Jesus, I cast myself down with my

face to the earth, and adore thee profoundly hidden in this sacrament of love. O God of love, I offer thee my poor heart in testimony of my reverence, adoration, and love. Eternal Father, look upon thy divine Son sacrificed upon this altar, and for his sake have mercy on me.

13. During the consecration of the precious blood and the elevation of the chalice, remain in profound silence, reverence, and interior recollection, believing that now the adorable Victim is immolated. Imagine that you see the heavens opening, and angels descending to adore their King and Lord in the sacred species; that God, at the sight of this offering, sends down a shower of graces upon the hearts of all those who are disposed to receive them—graces of sanctity for the just —graces of repentance for sinners. Finally, have confidence that you can obtain all things from God in these precious moments, through the passion and death of his blessed Son. Eternal Father, I offer thee the precious blood

of Jesus Christ in satisfaction for my sins. Eternal Father, through the precious blood of Jesus, save my soul. Eternal Father, through the precious blood of Jesus, have mercy on me.

14. After the *Elevation*, offer this adorable Victim for the four great ends of the eucharistic sacrifice, this being the principal devotion, and, withal, the most usual with those who hear Mass devoutly.

First, offer it for the glory of God, making acts of faith in his being your first beginning and last end. He is your King, your Creator, your Redeemer, your Sanctifier, your All. Renew your acts of hope, that he will pardon all your sins through the merits of Jesus Christ, sacrificed for you upon the altar; that he will give you paradise, will enrich you with his graces, and assist you in all your temporal and spiritual necessities. Repeat acts of charity, by offering yourself and giving yourself up entirely to God, to the fulfilment of his holy will and his designs concerning you. Excite yourself to a deep humility and abasement of yourself, in imitation of Jesus Christ, your head, who so lowers his majesty in this sacrament, offering to live and die for his glory. This is the first end of the sacrifice.

In the second place, offer this sacrifice to God in thanksgiving for all the benefits he has conferred upon you, as well general as particular, spiritual as temporal, and not only upon yourself but upon all men, especially those saints whom the Church commemorates on this day. Offer the body and the blood of Jesus Christ to the divine Father, to supply for your deficiency in gratitude.

In the third place, offer up this sacred Victim as a sacrifice of expiation for the sins of all men, and especially for those you have committed yourself or caused others to commit. There is no penance you may perform can equal the satisfaction you render to God with this great and adorable sacrifice, which is the same as that offered by Jesus Christ upon Calvary.

Lastly, offer it up in petition for all the graces necessary for the salvation of your soul, to obtain help and succour in all your own needs and those also of your neighbour. In order to help your memory, apply each of your petitions to one of the wounds of Jesus Christ, in this manner:—

Look with a lively faith upon Jesus hanging on the cross, and considering his divine head pierced with thorns, pray for holy Church, pray for the Pope, for your bishop, and generally for all ecclesiastical and secular superiors.

Considering the wound of his right hand, pray for your parents, benefactors, relations, and others recommended to your prayers.

At the wound in the left hand, pray for the enemies of the Church, for your own enemies, saying, with Christ on the cross, *Father, forgive them.*

At the wound in the right foot, pray for your inferiors, your servants, and generally for all those who in any way depend on you.

At the wound in the left foot, pray for

the conversion of sinners, for the holy souls in purgatory, especially for those for whom you are more obliged to pray, or have the greater need of your prayers.

When you come to the consideration of the wound in his sacred side, enter in spirit into the sacred heart pierced and opened for your love. Give yourself entirely to him, begging of him to fill you with his grace and spirit. Then ask of God, through the heart of Jesus, help in all your necessities, and especially the grace of a happy death; accept death when it may come for his glory and love, and in satisfaction for your sins.

15. This pious exercise ought to last till the *Agnus Dei*, when you ought to begin to prepare yourself for a spiritual communion, if you do not receive Jesus sacramentally, in ord r to participate the more abundantly in the fruits of the divine sacrifice.

16. At the communion of the priest, make an act of lively faith, an act of love towards Jesus veiled, an act of

contrition for your sins, and an ardent desire of receiving your God. Then imagining that you receive him invisibly from the hand of an angel, accept with love and reverence your sacramental Lord.

Let there be no Mass at which you assist in which you do not make a spiritual communion. Frequently do the same even out of Mass; it is very profitable to your spiritual advancement. Jesus Christ, by a wonderful humility and love, desires to unite himself to our souls; and for that end, hides his majesty under the accidents of bread: and shall we care but little about him, and have no great desire of receiving him? That is a coldness that grievously displeases him.

Spiritual Communion.—Most loving Jesus, I adore thee profoundly in this consecrated host, under the species of which I believe thee to be really present. I feel in my heart the sweet invitation thou givest me to approach and receive thee. But shall I not dread to open to thee, O Jesus, a heart so ill-disposed, so vicious, so unclean? Yet, this heart thou askest of me, and into this heart thou wishest to come and dwell. O love of my Jesus!

At least, O Lord, before coming, wash, with thy sacred blood, this heart of mine, cleanse it, purify it, sanctify it. I know my sins, my miseries; but then, as thou wishest to come and dwell in my heart, I open it to thee, I desire thee, I invite thee. Come, dear Jesus, come; my soul is anxious to possess thee. Come, delay not; I will welcome thee, embrace thee, and press thee to my heart. Thou art, and shalt be for ever, the God of my heart. Come and sanctify me with thy grace; cure me from my spiritual maladies; strengthen my weakness, infuse into me thy Spirit, inflame me with thy love, save this poor soul of mine which thou hast redeemed.

17. Continue in this holy exercise until the priest has read the prayers, adore your Lord, thank him humbly, and show him the wants of your soul.

18. When the priest has done the prayers, receive his blessing as you would that of God himself. Then thank God for the favour of having allowed you to assist at Mass, and ask

pardon for all the distractions and irreverences you have been guilty of during it.   My God, how many are deprived of the blessing of holy Mass, and I have had the privilege of assisting at it.   I thank thee for the favour. I beseech thee, O God, by the merits of Jesus Christ, who has been just offered to thee, to make me partaker in the fruits of his passion and precious blood.

19. Listen to the last Gospel with devotion and reverence, especially these words, *Verbum caro factum est*—the Word was made flesh—adoring the precious moment in which the Son of God became man for our love.   If you have received sacramentally, think that this divine incarnation has been repeated in a certain sense in yourself, and that Jesus Christ lives and dwells within you.

20. When Mass is over, renew the oblation of yourself once more, and declare that you will never commit a single sin.   Having left the church, deeply conscious of the greatness of

the mysteries you have been present at, keep a devout remembrance of them during the day, and zealously guard the heart you have given over and consecrated to Jesus Christ.

One of the following meditations may be profitably made during Mass, according to the devotion or inclination of the pious Christian.

CONSIDERATIONS ON THE PASSION OF JESUS CHRIST.

PERHAPS there is no subject of consideration more fitted for persons of every degree, than the passion and death of Jesus our Redeemer. Therein sinners find trust and encouragement for their conversion, and just souls assistance and strength for their progress in virtue. Therein all find consolation amid their efforts, patience in adversities, refuge in temptations, and every good unto their souls. Here, then, is the passion and death of our Redeemer drawn out for you in some brief considerations. You can make use of them for each day of the week; but let it not suffice you merely to glance over them with your eyes, nor read them in a passing way. Let your mind dwell on them with attention; endeavour to excite in your will such affections as are suggested by them, as of love, compassion, thankfulness, sorrow for sin, and the like. Pause upon such points as most impress you, and allow them to penetrate your heart. In this way you will prove by your own experience how useful it is to employ some little time every day in thinking upon the sufferings of our loving Redeemer.

Before meditating, never omit to make the acts of preparation pointed out at pp. 5 and 6, and to conclude it with some resolution, and a colloquy.

SUNDAY.

CONSIDERATION.—*Jesus' suffering merits our love and compassion.*

POINT I.—A God dies amidst boundless sufferings and pains for mankind. How powerful a motive to oblige us to the tenderest compassion, to the strongest love! Who is this God who submits to so many racking tortures? And men, what are they, that a God should suffer for them thus? My soul, this thought should absorb your affections. God is Greatness itself, is infinite Majesty itself, is infinite Omnipotence. Man is misery itself, baseness itself, a most vile nothing, a heap of sins. And yet, for love of this wretched nothingness, Jesus, the great Son of God, sacrifices His precious life, and with vehemence of love and of agony, expires transfixed upon a cross. Ah! how should we not love a God so loving, nor compassionate a God so tortured for his love to men? God so greatly desires the heart of man, that to gain it he spends the infinite treasure of his own blood. God so greatly thirsts for man's salvation, that to purchase it he reckons as cheaply spent a life of toils, of sufferings—a death of shame and pain. And thou, O my soul, wilt thou remain hard and unfeeling, with such tender proofs of the love of thy God in love with thee? Wilt thou not melt with feelings of love and compassion? Canst thou then compassionate a creature that suffers though not for thee, and yet for Jesus, who suffers, agonizes, dies for love of thee, wilt thou be quite without feeling? Shalt thou have a heart to love the earth, the world, creatures, and no heart to love Jesus agonising, Jesus dying for the love of men?

Ah! my dear Jesus, love of my soul, tell me, I beseech thee, wherefore suffer so much for me? Wherefore shed the last drop of thy precious blood? Wherefore sacrifice thy life? I understand, O Lord, in order to be loved by me, to be compassionated by me. O love! O love! And I shall go so far in my ingratitude as to deny thee my love? Never, my dear Jesus, never. I shall love thee henceforward with all my power, I shall feel for thy sufferings from the very depth of my heart; this I promise, O Lord; this, with thy help, I shall perform.

POINT II.—A God put to pain—a God put to death for man. This has always been, to pious souls, the sweetest and most abiding thought; this has been always the most forcible and pressing motive for bringing their hearts to the love of the suffering Jesus. This thought—*a God put to death for man*—will be the great cause of the confusion and despair of the damned in hell. A God has endured outrages and torments for my salvation! A God has bought heaven for me at the price of his blood, and I burn in these flames! Thus will the damned cry out in the abyss. How can I possibly doubt of his goodness and his love? My wickedness alone has been my eternal perdition, and an eternity of pains is too little to punish the monstrous ingratitude, with which I have corresponded to the love of a God, who has undergone for me such atrocious pains and so cruel a death. My soul, if thou refusest now to love and be grateful to a God, torn and blood-exhausted for thee on a cross, deservedly wilt thou burn in the everlasting flames of hell. Wouldst thou rather choose these tormenting flames, than the sweet flames of charity and love for thy suffering God? Ah, no; resolve to consecrate thy whole heart to this loving Redeemer, who sacrificed himself wholly for thy salvation. Fix the eyes of thy mind upon thy crucified Lord, and say to thyself: Behold a God upon this cross for the love of me and for my benefit! Behold his wounds, so many mouths pleading piteously for compassion and love!

Most amiable Lord, ah! for pity, enkindle in my heart one spark of charity, one small sentiment of compassion for thee. Let it never be said, my dear Redeemer, that this soul of mine, which has cost thee so many pains, and which thou hast bought back at so dear a price, is lost. Too justly do I deserve hell for not having loved thee, and for having lived so forgetful of thee and thy sufferings; but henceforth, O Lord, thou wilt be the sole object of my love—thou and thy bitter passion, the objects most dear to me, the subject of my meditations, and the centre of my affections. Yes, I shall do so my dear Redeemer, and do thou engrave deeply upon my heart thy most bitter pains.

Point III.—Consider that Jesus has suffered a most bitter passion and a cruel death for his very enemies, for most ungrateful rebels, for faithless traitors. This reflection, O my soul, is a new motive which ought to compel thee still more to compassionate and love your crucified Lord. If the dying for a friend is a proof of most perfect charity, what excess of love does he not show who dies for vile, unrequiting, and audacious enemies? See the point at which the love of Jesus has arrived. He shed his blood through his wounds, he drained his veins upon the cross for those who cared not for him, and made outrages and offences the return to so much love. Wouldst thou be one of those, my soul, for whom Jesus died, and who ceased not even after he was dead to pierce his most loving heart! Jesus saw thy disregard; he recognized thee as an enemy; he considered thee as his tormentor, yet he would not give up his loving intention of suffering and dying for thee. He saw thy monstrous callousness to love after so much goodness, nevertheless he would not prevent thee from enjoying so many times the plentiful fruits of his love and of his passion. Nay, he wanted to show thee the excess of his love by means of a death the most infamous and the most painful. Ah! rouse yourself for once to a correspondence with such an extraordinary proof of love. Resolve for once to detach your heart from earth, from vanity, and from sin, to give it to your agonizing Saviour. Can you give him less than your love and compassion? Can you have the heart to deny him this?

My dear Jesus, what can I say at the sight of so much love, of so many pains by which thou intendest to gain my love? Nought else but that thy goodness is infinite. But what shall I say at the sight of my own perfidy, by which I never ceased to offend one who loved me so much? O God, infinitely good, I detest my own wickedness, notwithstanding which I have been still so dear to thy eyes. I am disgusted at myself for having lived forgetful of thee, and of the sufferings endured for me. Never, dear Redeemer, never shall I be ungrateful to thee again. Do thou confirm this good resolution I have formed of loving and compassionating thee as long as I live. I promise it to thee, dear Jesus; and to give thee an earnest of its genuineness, I dedicate myself this very day to meditating continually on thy most bitter passion.

Pious Practice and Fruit.

Renew to-day the resolution of often calling to mind the sufferings of Jesus Christ. Be careful in the little troubles that come across you to offer them to God in union with the passion of his Son. Say often from your heart: *My Jesus, I suffer for love of thee.* Have recourse in all your afflictions to Jesus suffering, and compassionate his pains. Say to him that you wish to find therein all your consolation; thank your divine Redeemer frequently for the great love he bears towards you, and for what he has suffered for the love of you.

MONDAY.

CONSIDERATION.—*Jesus' Agony in the Garden.*

POINT I.—Jesus having entered the garden of Gethsemane, there to begin his sorrowful passion, falls prostrate on the ground, and begins his prayer. Approach, my soul, thy blessed Redeemer, and meditate on the unspeakable anguish that tries his spirit in this prayer. Sad images, appalling scenes, press upon him, and lay siege to every avenue of his divine heart. His soul is assailed by a mortal sadness, and by such painful agonies as the human mind cannot conceive. Tormenting fears, sorrowful thoughts, and bitter anguish rend him interiorly. The most afflicted Jesus, being reduced to such a pitiable state, raises his tearful eyes to heaven, and asks for some little comfort from his divine Father ; he turns to his disciples: my dear children, he says, I am sorrowful even unto death, do not abandon me. The attack upon him reaches its height, and being no longer able to hold out against such ineffable griefs, his face grows pale, he faints, and falls into a mortal agony. My soul, do thou at least come to console thy agonizing Redeemer; run with some feelings of love and compassion to bring some comfort for his afflictions.

R

O Jesus, delight of the saints, joy of paradise, consoler of the afflicted, wherefore endure such sorrow, an agony so painful? Jesus brings himself to this, in order to merit consolation for us in our troubles, strength in our labours, and the endless joys of heaven. What goodness, what love of Jesus for us! And thou, wilt thou not love him? Wilt thou not undertake to suffer something for love of him? To drink one drop of that dolorous chalice Jesus has drained for thee?

Ah! my dear Jesus, can I ever be forgetful of thy love and of thy agonies? Can I ever thank thee sufficiently, O loving Saviour, for the mortal anguish thy soul has been pleased to endure for love of me? Ah! for pity's sake, cause thy sufferings to be so deeply impressed upon my soul, that I cannot possibly forget them. Do thou encourage my heart, weak as it is, and slack in the pains and troubles of my life, to the end that, suffering with thee, I may be also a sharer in thy glory.

Point II.—Consider what were the painful objects that united, like so many cruel executioners, to martyr the afflicted heart of Jesus. The first and most appaling were our sins. The vivid knowledge of all the sins of men, a thorough sight of their enormity, a most intense horror of their shocking malignity, filled his heart, pressed upon it with such piercing intensity, as to produce a sorrow and a sadness that cannot be imagined. Jesus knows, measures, and comprehends the entire malice and atrocity of sin, the enormity of the insult thereby offered to his heavenly Father; and, loving his Father with a supreme love, he experiences a grief so poignant, a horror so excessive of human wickedness—all this pourtrayed before him in its deformed ugliness—that he is ready to expire for sheer broken-heartedness. The sins, then, of all men, past, present, and to come, were the cruel tormentors which tore without pity the sad heart of our agonizing Redeemer in sunder.

He feels them one by one, one by one they afflict and grieve him. My soul, what share had thy misdeeds in embittering the heart of thy Jesus? Those sins that seemed to thee once so sweet, agonized thy Jesus with unalloyed grief. Those sins thou hast committed in fun, in play, for nothing, have barbarously rent the heart of Jesus: His sadness, his anguish, his agony, were increased by thy sins, by the malice of thy iniquities. He saw all, and since they were the sins of a Christian soul, by how much the more it were loved and cherished by him, by so much the more did the enormity of its ingratitude afflict him. Oh! how much the less would Jesus have suffered, hadst thou but sinned less. Ah! weep scalding tears now for thy crimes, detest thy malice, and resolve never more to offend so loving a Redeemer.

My sorrowing, agonizing Jesus, my faults, yes, my misdeeds, have brought thee to so pitiable a state, the sad state in which I behold thee. And yet I do not cease offending thee. I have not given up tearing thy most sacred heart with my sins. I torment this heart, so dear, so amiable; which burns with love for me, although I have not had for thee but disregard and contempt. Ah! why does not this heart of mine burst at the sight of its own perfidy? Dear Jesus, give me tears of real sorrow, that I may weep for my sins whilst I live; and give me the grace never more to return to those sins that have cost thee so much.

POINT III.—Consider how the impending passion of the Son of God, which was to work such a fearful carnage on his body, concurred in tormenting his innocent soul in the garden. The loving impatience which Jesus had to suffer for us, made him invent this unheard-of expedient of forestalling, in order to bear collectively, those pains and sorrows, that were to rack him so unmercifully, one by one, afterwards. All the fearful torments which human malice is devising against

him, flit before his mind at once.   The
insults, the mockeries, the opprobria,
the blasphemies with which he is to be
maltreated by his own people, are de-
picted to the life in their most telling
form, before his imagination, and
cause him the deepest possible concern. He sees the buffets, the chains,
the scourges, the thorns, the nails, the
cross upon which, saturated with injuries, in the midst of infinite agony,
and between two thieves, he is to die:
he understands all its horrible bar-
barity, and experiences therefrom
the most bitter pain.   To-morrow,
he says to himself, to-morrow this
body of mine, torn, weltering, exhausted, will hang from an infamous gibbet.   My flesh will be
covered with livid sores, with wounds,
and be torn by scourges.   Oh! what
a horrible torture, what a fearful
butchery does this anticipated cruelty
make of his divine heart, as it lies
buried in such a deluge of woes.
Jesus, having entered deeply into the
meditation on all his sorrows, collects

together the most painful, and scatters them over his afflicted spirit. At such a sight, the interior pains of Jesus are so excessive, that he trembles, grows pale, falls to the earth, and getting into a deathlike agony, streams of blood sweat forth from the pores of his most sacred body. Stay, my soul, to collect, reverently and lovingly, this precious blood, which floods the earth, in order to form therewith a bath for my uncleanness. Meditate how ingenuous has been the love of Jesus, when it made him the executioner of his own divine heart, by so wonderful an invention of suffering. Condole with him in these untold sufferings, and if he makes unheard-of and unusual efforts to suffer still more, thereby to prove the love he bears thee, do thou render love for love. Ah! love a God so loving.

Ah! ardent lover of my soul, agonizing for me, I adore thee, I love thee, I thank thee. I kiss this divine blood, which the excessive anguish of thy heart has pressed out of thy veins.

Oh! that it would but fall on the unclean earth of my heart, to wash it, and inflame it with love for thee! I wish to love thee, I wish to be thine, and suffer for thee, since I see thee so desirous and greedy of pains for my sake. But, ah! by the merits of that precious blood which thou hast shed in the garden, create in me a new heart, a heart that may have no other affections than those of love, of compassion, and of gratitude for thee, my most loving and loveable Redeemer.

Pious Practice and Fruit.

Try every day to keep with your heart near Jesus praying in the garden. Compassionate him often in his sorrowful agony. Offer his prayer to the divine Father, beseeching that for its sake he may pardon you the many deficiencies of your own prayers. Deprive yourself of some amusement for the sake of Jesus agonizing in the garden. Resolve, at the sight of a God sweating blood for you, to encounter with pleasure the difficulties you may meet in the observance of his law, and in the avoiding of sin.

TUESDAY.

Jesus Scourged at the Pillar.

POINT I.—Prepare thyself, my soul, for affliction and tears, as thou comest to contemplate the frightful tortures practised on thy Redeemer. Enter a moment, in thought, into the hall of Pilate, and look at that innocent Lamb given up to the rabid ferocity and inhuman fury of those merciless butchers, to be tormented by them. O God, what a cruel carnage is made of the virginal flesh of the Son of God! A shower of most furious blows rains down upon every spot of his immaculate body, from heavy lashes; with such ferocity do they strike, that, digging into his sacred members, they plough up his flesh, they wrench the arteries, they tear the veins, and open wounds in every part, and tear and strike into the very wounds again and again. What spectacle has heaven seen more pitiful than this! Ah! why, my heart, dost thou not break in pieces in seeing thy God made thus a man of sorrows? From the sole of his foot to the crown of his head, he is all torn and wounded. The blood gushes out on every side in rivers, and already the pavement is covered with it; it is bespattered upon the monsters themselves, who cease not to strike their fainting Lord. Look, my soul, at thy Jesus, thy Father, thy God, torn, bleeding, and all but expiring, through the horrible torture inflicted. See if there be any suffering like to his, and shed one tear of compassion over so many pains. Look, and read in these wounds the love that Jesus bears to thee, and conclude from this blood how much thou hast cost him.

O my most loving Redeemer, my most patient Jesus, has the loving of me cost thee so much? Hast thou purchased my soul at such a price? I kiss with deep compassion thy wounds, and adore most reverently the blood thou hast shed so copiously for me. I feel for thee, in the sad state in which I behold thee, all disfigured in thy immaculate body, and torn so unmercifully with the cruel scourges. Graciously deign, dear Saviour, to impress upon my heart lively sentiments of love and compassion for thy sufferings, so that I may never forget what thou hast endured for me, and never cease to bewail my sins, which have caused thee so much grief.

POINT II.—Consider, my soul, the feelings of the loving heart of Jesus in the midst of the pains of his scourging. To the savageness, to the cruelty, of his torturers, so thirsty for his blood, Jesus opposes nought save a patience, a meekness, and a silence quite astonishing. Thy blessed Saviour stands bound to a pillar, under a deluge of stripes, like an innocent victim upon an altar, offering to his divine Father his blood, his pains, his wounds for me. He has me then before his mind, seems utterly taken up with loving me, and forming from his own veins a bath of salvation for the mortal wounds of my soul. He feels the full pain of his wounds, but his love cannot say enough; his thirst is only increased to suffer still more. What dost thou say, my soul, in reflecting on thy own delicacy, which will not endure a slight inconvenience, a little pain, for one who has endured so much for the love he bears thee? Jesus sees with what hatred, with what injustice, his enemies make such havoc on his sacred body; nevertheless, he does not utter one word of complaint or blame: he is wholly engrossed in offering to his Father his ignominy and torments for their very sakes. He turns his pitiful looks now to the earth, now to heaven, to beg with their entreating expression mercy from his eternal Father for the grievous sins I have committed. Behold, my soul, how Jesus suffers, and what.an example he gives thee of suffering profitably! See how much thou art bound to so loving a heart, which, in the midst of torments so excessive, only loves thee the more tenderly.

I thank thee, O sweet Jesus, with my whole soul, for the pains thou hast endured for me in thy scourging, and endured with so much patience and love. O Lord, great, indeed, is the love thou bearest me; ardent, indeed, is the desire thou hast of my salvation. Ah! grant that I may correspond with thy wishes; grant that so much blood be not shed for me in vain; grant, for pity's sake, grant, that I may save my soul, which thou hast loved so intensely. Make me, dear Jesus, like thee in patience, in humility, in long-suffering; give me grace to embrace, with the spirit of true penance, whatever shall happen to me painful or afflictive; let me always bear thee in mind, who hast suffered so much to satisfy for my sins.

Point III.—Ask, my soul, of the eternal Father, why he has left his beloved Son at the mercy of his cruel torturers? He will answer thee in the words of Isaias: "*for the wickedness of my people I have struck him.*" On account of the sins of men it was that

I allowed my Son to submit himself to such tortures. Ask, my soul, the suffering Jesus himself, why have so many scourges of the divine justice fallen upon him; and he will answer thee in the words of the prophet, that he had to satisfy for our iniquity, and take upon himself the punishment due to sinners. Dost thou wish to know how enormous thy sins must be? Look at Jesus torn and bleeding under the scourges. See what streams of blood this Man-God had to pour out in order to blot them out, and appease the divine wrath they had provoked. The sins of impurity especially were those which made the most fearful tortures on the immaculate and sinless body of the Son of God. These were the most cruel and inhuman tormentors of his virginal flesh. Aye, those guilty gratifications I have so often allowed my lustful body—those unworthy pleasures by which I have so often trampled on the law of God—those immodesties by which I have ensnared the innocence of others, have cost Jesus the atrocious pains, the shameful confusion of his scourging. In order to pay, O my heart, for thy guilty complacency, for thy evil delights, Jesus is bruised by those blows, which furrow and tear in pieces his sinless flesh. O sins, O pleasures, O impurities, what have you not cost my Saviour! My pleasure has had no restraint; and without bounds, without measure, has been the ignominy, the shame, the pains of the incarnate Son of God. I have deserved the strokes, but Jesus took them on himself to merit me pardon and salvation. Ah! when wilt thou resolve, my soul, after contemplating thy Saviour torn in all his members, to chastise thy flesh, which has been thy instrument and servant in so many sins?

And who was it, O loving Saviour, that has so cruelly macerated thy innocent flesh? And for what fault of thine hast thou been so barbarously scourged? Ah! I see. Thou hast endured the penalty of my sins; I am the guilty one, and thou hast been punished.   My sins against thee have sharpened, my sins have formed those lashes that lacerated thy body.   For the sake of that precious blood thou hast shed so plentifully, grant me, dear Jesus, a true sorrow for my sins; give me tears of sincere compunction to weep for my wickedness; grant me the firm resolution never again to repeat thy cruel pains.

Pious Practice and Fruit.

In remembrance and in honour of the scourging of Jesus Christ, find out to-day some kind of penance or mortification for your body, punishing thereby your flesh in something.   At least, receive with submission and patience some ill-fortune, which may come to-day as a scourge God uses to chastise you for your sins.   Conceive a holy hatred against your flesh, which, by ministering to your sinful desires, has cost Jesus so much.   Make a law for yourself to deny yourself some satisfaction to-day for his sake.

WEDNESDAY.

CONSIDERATION.—*Jesus crowned with Thorns.*

POINT I.—Consider how, the scourging over, Jesus is not allowed one moment of rest, but one torment succeeds another in racking our suffering Lord. Of all his body, the head alone has remained not much injured by the barbarous scourging. The executioners adverting to this, with unheard-of cruelty, resort to an invention—oh! how painful!—in order to make him—now weak and dying—the very King of sorrows. They take a bundle of sharp thorns, and platting them together in the shape of a crown, they place them on his sacred head. Then they pitilessly press them down with repeated blows, the points enter in, and, piercing the flesh and the nerves, cause spasms of pain to our blessed Jesus. Oh! what a horrible garland is this, my heart, and what intense pains must it cause the adorable head of our Redeemer. A thorn that chances to enter the foot of a lion, makes him roar and bellow: what torment must Jesus have endured from so many sharp thorns pressed with such force into his sacred head! Stop, my soul, to consider and compassionate this King of sorrows. Men generally study new and exquisite ways for sinful delights, and for Jesus are invented exquisite ways of torture, in order that he by pouring out his blood such a way could atone for the manner of sinning as well as the sin itself, thus to extinguish in man the lamentable thirst for pleasure. My soul, wilt thou go and crown thyself with roses after beholding thy God crowned with thorns? Wilt thou refuse him some light suffering when he has been satiated with pains for thee? Ah! for once be ashamed of living in delicacy and sin, whilst thou sees thy King pierced with thorns.

O my Jesus, the most aggrieved of all men, and the greatest of all kings,

I acknowledge thee as the only true king of my heart. I render thee the most profound homage, as due to thee as my God and my Lord.

Ah! by right, it is not on thine, but on my proud and guilty head, ought to be placed those thorns which pierced thy adorable temples. Yet, O most innocent Saviour, thou wouldst have thyself crowned with thorns, in order that thou mightest crown me with glory. I thank thee, O my God; and in order to become like thee, I shall try to endure the punctures of the troubles and tribulations of the present life. I renounce for ever pastimes and delights of earth, in order to follow Thee, suffering Redeemer.

Point II.—His tormentors, not content with deriding and insulting, by their buffoonery and blasphemy, our afflicted Redeemer, and making him the butt of their inhuman sport, they hurl hard blows upon his divine countenance, and cover his face with filthy spittle. Behold this most meek lamb in the midst of these ravening wolves

—his humble deportment—his cast-down look—beaming with the most wonderful patience and profound humility, the greatest ignominies the perfidy of men can invent and offer. To the mockeries, the insults, and the buffets, they add heavy blows upon his adorable head, with which they press in and break the thorns, wounding him so deeply, that our suffering Lord cannot but endure the most fearful torture it is possible to conceive. The thorns deeply penetrate the head, they force out rivulets of blood, which runs down upon his forehead, closes his eyes, and defaces his benign and heavenly countenance. Meditate, O my soul, upon this fearful torture of the sacred head of Jesus, and keep thyself, if thou canst, from being moved with compassion for thy Father and Lord, who suffers thus for thy sake. Oh, who can express what he suffers! Yet he endures all without a word of complaint. He turns his pitiful look towards his hard-hearted tormentors, in testimony of his excessive love, and to appeal through them to all men to give his sufferings one look of compassion. See, he seems to say, how far your pride, your excess of vanity and pleasure, must have gone, if I had to endure all this in order to atone for them. See if I do not claim at least one sigh, one tear of pity, after I have shed so much blood, through the scourges and thorns, for the love I bear for you, and through my desire to satisfy for your sins.

Yes, dear Jesus, thou art worthy of all our pity and all our love, and I cannot help giving mine when I see thee in this condition for my sake. I reverence those thorns which crown thee with ignominy and pain, and were so dear to thee, because they declared thee King of sorrows. I am ashamed of myself, when, with thy example before me, I seek after nothing but pleasures and comforts. I wish to be considered a member of thy body, and yet I dread and fly with caution from the pains which thou, my head, hast suffered so willingly. Alas!

what insolence! vile worm that I am, having merited every kind of penalty for my sins, wish to be crowned with roses and satiated with delights, whilst beholding thee, my King, my God, with a piercing diadem of thorns upon thy head. I beseech thee, my dear Redeemer, to detach my heart, by thy grace, from vanity and earthly affections; give me a love for suffering; make me enamoured of thee who meritest all my love.

Point III.—Consider why Jesus wished to be crowned with thorns. It was to blot out, by new shedding of blood, our sins of thought especially. He came down from heaven to wash out sin by his blood, to satisfy for them by his passion, and to abolish them by his death. The source of sin is the head; then are formed thoughts of impurity, of ambition, of injustice, of hatred, of revenge. It was meet, therefore, that his sacred head should pay their penalty by new ignominy and new pain. The love of Jesus could not allow this noble part of his sacred body to be without its particular torture. Hence it is that he willingly submits it to the piercing of the thorns, to this new and unheard-of torment, on account of our wicked thoughts. See, my soul, if there be a single part of the divine head of Jesus not torn and pierced. See how this innocent victim, destined to be immolated for thy sins, is entirely consumed by the fire of suffering. Recognize in these cruel thorns, which transfix his sacred head, the wicked work of thy sinful thoughts. These have formed a more painful crown for Jesus' head than the thorns themselves. For these transfix the heart, the very soul, of Jesus, with the most intense pangs of agony. The thoughts of vanity, of self-conceit, of pride, of impurity, which have so often been formed and encouraged in thy mind, were the cruel tormentors of the head of thy Jesus. Ah! my heart, weep for grief, and pour out a torrent of tears over thy sins; weep also with compassion and love for thy Saviour, who has paid so dearly for thy misdeeds. But, oh! never return to those abominable thoughts, which are so many additional thorns in Jesus' crown, and pierce anew his loving heart.

What a pitiable figure have my sins reduced thee to, O my Jesus! Oh! to see thee disfigured, lacerated, pierced with thorns, covered with blood, my sweet Redeemer! Alas! what evil have I done by sinning, what harm by these sinful thoughts, when by them I have crowned with thorns, with ignominy, with tortures, thy most sacred head! Ah! my most amiable Saviour, I am displeased above everything at having sinned; but, ah! do have pity on me and pardon me. I am resolved never to repeat my offences; but do thou aid me in keeping my mind free from evil thoughts, so that I may the more easily preserve thy grace in my soul, and never have the misfortune to cause thee displeasure. I ask this favour of thee through the pains thou hast endured in thy coronation, and through the blood that has flowed from thy sacred head.

Pious Practice and Fruit.

Conceive a great horror for vanity in every shape. Cut short at once the train of evil thoughts, by turning your mind to consider the pains caused by the thorns to Jesus' sacred head. When you come across something that annoys you, when you are displeased or dis-comfited, say to yourself: *Do I want to be a delicate member under a head crowned with thorns? This is a little thorn from the crown of Jesus, which he sends me to make me a sharer in his suffering.*

THURSDAY.

CONSIDERATION.—*Jesus takes up his Cross, and goes to Calvary.*

POINT I.—The unjust sentence of death is scarcely pronounced by the wicked judge against our innocent Saviour, when his enemies show the utmost eagerness to carry it into execution. 'Having put together, in a short time, a large and heavy cross, they present it to the suffering and almost expiring Jesus as the instrument of his ignominious passion. Meditate, my soul, with what thoughts our Saviour looks on, and with what feelings he embraces this painful gibbet. The cross has always been the dear object of the desires of his loving heart. He has had all along a loving impatience to terminate his mortal life upon the cross for love of us. Now, on seeing it offered to him, these desires are not changed; nay, he receives it with a complacent heart, he fixes his eyes upon it and to it, as to his dearest treasure; he desires to be united, and to die finally in its embrace. Enter into the heart of Jesus, and see what thanks he offers his divine Father for having prepared for him a throne upon which, satiated with ignominies, he can extinguish the ardent thirst he has of suffering and dying for men. Observe with what love, with what zest he stretches forth his hands to embrace his beloved cross; he presses it, kisses it, places it on his tired and bleeding shoulders, that thereby he may convince us of the exquisite perfection of his love for us. What dost thou say, my soul, at the sight of a love so strong, so generous, in Jesus, for the cross? Thou troublest and vexest thyself at the slightest inconvenience. Thou shrinkest from a little labour, and fliest from or refusest the little crosses Jesus, from time to time, presenteth to thee. What resemblance canst thou ever claim to Jesus crucified, so enamoured of the cross, if there be nothing seen in thee but an abhorrence for suffering and mortification? Ah! unite thyself with Jesus, in embracing the cross of troubles and afflictions, of evils and tribulations, all sanctified by Jesus having embraced his cross.

Oh! my most loving Jesus, has the malice of man, and my cold-hearted ingratitude, offered thee nought but the disgraceful gibbet of the cross?

For thee, however, the love thou hast for me, and the thirst with which thou art burning for my salvation, is enough to make Thee look upon it with a transport of joy, and embrace it with delight.   Ah! what a love is thine, my Jesus!   Not yet content with having endured so much, shed so much blood, still so ardently longs to be immolated on the cross!   What portion can I ever claim with thee, whilst the cross, which to thy heart is so dear, is so abhorrent to me?   If I loved thee, O divine Love, I would also love suffering; but since I love thee not, I, hate suffering so much.   Ah! grant that I may love thee, and let my love of the cross, for the future, be a testimony thereof.   I wish to embrace it, I wish to carry it, and if, for love of thee, I ought to die upon the cross, willingly do I sacrifice myself to a death that was so dear to thee.

POINT II.—The executioners, impatient to see the loving, and yet so much hated, Lord nailed to the cross, having loaded him with its weight,

and bound him with ropes and chains,
they hastily drag him along from ungrateful Jerusalem to Calvary. Follow
with thy heart and mind your suffering
Jesus in his painful journey, and with
sentiments of tender compassion, bear
him company. He, though fainting
and weary by his agony, by the loss of
so much blood, by so many stripes and
blows, all torn and wounded, does not
refuse to follow, with his heavy load,
his enemies, who hurry him up the
hill. They are very anxious to see
him die soon, but much stronger is
Jesus' desire of sacrificing himself upon
the altar of the cross for our love.
Our beloved Saviour proceeds, and
although every step causes him new
torture, yet, conquering by his charity
the weakness of his flesh, he goes on
very fast. He must feel terrible confusion at having to appear before an
immense crowd of people, drawn together in order to gaze at the noto-
rious malefactor, between two thieves,
who are to be his companions in suffering—yet he does not halt. Oh! how

confounded ought you be with shame, you, who for human respect, for a joke or a jest, abandon the path of virtue, and give up good works and the following of Jesus Christ! Consider, O my heart, how the whole way through which Jesus passes is stained with blood, until he is completely exhausted, and cannot go further. To such a pitiful state is he reduced, that one single look at him is enough to move the most stony of hearts, and draw tears from the eye. But thou, reflecting on this, art cold and insensible towards Jesus, who is so pained in his galling journey. The cross he bears is painful, heavy, and unjust, and yet he cheerfully carries it, and goes inviting thee to carry your cross after him to paradise. No cross will ever be so weighty or painful for thee as that of Jesus was. Wilt thou, then, refuse to accept it from his hands? Wilt thou shrink from bearing it in his company? Without the cross, the way to heaven is not open to thee; without the cross, thou canst not be a follower of Jesus. Courage, then, and follow in his footsteps with cheerfulness. Do not fear that he will not lighten its weight; he will cheer thee and assist thee.

I consecrate to thee from this moment, O most loving Redeemer, my liberty, and give it to thee, to be ready to bear whatever cross thou shalt be pleased to send me. I accept willingly, and submit my soul to the cross of thy divine law; be it severe, be it hard, be it heavy, no matter, I shall bear it by a faithful observance. It is enough, and more than enough, that hitherto I have refused, by shaking off its sweet yoke. I am sick of my past delicacy; it made me heedless to follow thee in the way of the Gospel, and in the observance of thy precepts. Assist me by thy grace, so that the difficulties may not deter me, nor draw me back from doing what I ought, and what I now promise to perform. I wish to follow thee everywhere, wherever it is thy pleasure to conduct me.

O dear Jesus, since thou hast borne thy cross, so painful and so heavy, I wish to take mine also on my shoulders, and carry it after thee, in order that I may come with thee to the blessed gate of paradise.

Point III.—Jesus tottering under the heavy weight of his cross, and no longer able, from sheer weariness and faintness, as well as the painfulness of his sores, to hold out, he falls under its weight. Oh! how much have those strayed steps, you have so often made in the ways of iniquity and sin, cost Jesus? But, at least, a feeling of human compassion moved the hearts of his enemies to give some relief to their fallen Lord or help kindly to rise. No; all pity, compassion, and sympathy, for Jesus, has long since been extinguished in them. On the contrary, with barbarous fury, they kick him, they strike him, and try every manner of cruelty, to make him rise from the ground, and make him prosecute his journey to his greater torment, amid jeers, insults, and blows. His love for us, his desire to die and atone for our sins, imparts strength to him, and invigorates his body, already exhausted; and it seems to him as if the hour was long in coming, when he was to expire on Calvary for our redemption. The weight of the cross bows him down the more, pains and galls his wounded shoulders; every minute he gets weaker, and yet he gets no pity from the inhuman hearts of his enemies. He will find some from you, at least, who has had so much to do in tormenting him with thy irregular desires. If you saw a malefactor led to execution, you would be kindly disposed towards him, and give him some evidence of your pity—how much more ought you be softened at seeing Jesus led to death—to the death of the cross? Jesus, the most innocent, the most amiable, and the most holy of men! Jesus, the Son of God, who goes to suffer, for love of you, a death the most cruel, infamous, and ignominious, that can possibly be conceived; who goes, carrying upon

T

his shoulders the heavy cross. Jesus has a heavy weight to bear in the cross; but far more heavy is the weight of our sins placed upon him by his divine Father. This is the weight which, of all others, weakens and oppresses him. Wouldst thou wish to know, my soul, the greatness of thy sins? See a God-man fainting and falling under his cross. Ah! compassionate thy Jesus; weep for, and detest thy sins, which have weighed so heavily on thy Redeemer, and have caused him so much pain on his way to Calvary. If thou hadst not sinned, Jesus would not have borne so heavy a cross— he would have had a much lighter load. Thou hast, therefore, added to his burden. Ah! do not be so cruel and inhuman towards thy Jesus, as to renew his cross again by thy sins.

O most loving Jesus, thou art the true Son of God, the adorable Creator of heaven and earth—infinitely great and powerful. How is it, therefore, that thou languishest and fallest under the weight of the cross? O Lord, what a terrible evil must sin be, since, when placed on thy divine shoulders, it makes thee fall to the earth for very horror! The cross weighed thee down only when on the way to Calvary; but my sins have weighed on thee night and day during the whole of thy mortal life, paining thee with their deformity, and present to thy mind in all their ugliness. I am sorry for having committed them; and would to God they had never been committed! I thank thee for having, with so much love, taken upon thyself the burden of my sins, to free me from the chastisement due to them. I love thee, O loving Lord; I love thee, my amiable Redeemer; I wish always to love thee, and never more to offend thee.

Pious Practice and Fruit.

Put before you all the crosses which God could send you, and offer yourself willingly to embrace them for the love of Jesus Christ. In thy sufferings do not lose sight of Jesus, who carries so painful and heavy a cross, and beg of him to communicate to you a share in his spirit. Examine to-day if all thy steps be taken in the way of the divine law and of virtue; and if you find yourself deviating therefrom, resolve efficaciously to walk constantly in the footsteps of Jesus Christ. Keep thy ways from every place in which a stumbling-block might be found to thy innocence, or the danger of offending God.

FRIDAY.

CONSIDERATION—*Jesus nailed to the Cross.*

POINT I.—The sorrowful Jesus having arrived with extreme difficulty on Calvary, the executioners strip him of his clothes, tearing them violently from his sacred body, to which they had been stuck closely by the wounds and clotted blood. Meditate, O my soul, what pain must have been caused to our suffering Lord in opening his wounds in this manner. Then say to thyself: Behold the rest that is given to my suffering Redeemer, after so long and painful a journey! See the comfort they provide for him before his cruel crucifixion! Jesus, the victim destined for the sacrifice, having received orders to lie down upon the gibbet prepared for him, in obedience and silence lays his bleeding body upon the altar of the cross, and sweetly presents his hands and feet to be nailed to this rough bed of death. Observe, O Christian soul, thy Redeemer, how he raises his eyes to heaven, and with sublime sentiments of humility and submission, offers himself in sacrifice to his eternal Father for thy salvation. Oh! how much dost thou owe Jesus; and at the same time how ungrateful and insensible art thou in return! The torturers draw near, and with rough nails, by the blows of heavy hammers, they pierce through the hands and feet of our beloved Redeemer. The spasms of pain that Jesus then endured at this new torture, cannot be described for intensity; they can only be wept at and felt for. His flesh is dug open in awful wounds; the nerves, the veins, the arteries are wrenched. The more the nails are driven the wider are the wounds made, until four rivers of blood flow from his hands and feet, to wash our souls from the filth of sin. In what, my soul, have these hands and feet of thy dear Jesus sinned, that they should be subject to such torture? Ask not the innocent Jesus, but ask thyself. On account of thy wicked and sinful actions, on account of the steps thou hast taken in the way of evil, Jesus' hands and feet are pierced. To satisfy for the abuse thou hast made of thy liberty, Jesus is nailed to the cross. Look upon thy Saviour fixed to this hard wood, to which the vehemence of his love for thee and obedience to his divine Father, far more than the nails, keep him attached. Ah! if thou hadst loved thy God, thou wouldst have subjected thyself to the hardest obedience, thou wouldst not have violated his holy law, thou wouldst have crucified thy rebellious flesh by mortification and penance, rather than offend thy Lord and Father. Resolve to-day, at the foot of the crucifix, to do so.

I adore thee, O loving Redeemer, upon this throne of love and pain, where I see thee lacerated and blood-exhausted. I cast myself into thy loving arms, since I see them open to embrace me. I embrace thy cross, which is to thee an altar of obedience to the command of thy divine Father, and to me a throne of grace and mercy. Shall it ever be possible, O God of infinite love and majesty, that I can think of thee humbled to the ignominy of the cross, in order to teach me, and impress upon my heart the virtue of obedience, and that I, a vile sinner, should refuse to obey thee the Sovereign Lord of all! Ah! dear Jesus, grant me to love warmly the obeying of thee and thy precepts, and the having thy most holy will as the rule of my every action. Grant me to understand thoroughly this great truth, that all my happiness consists in pleasing thee, and in faithfully observing thy wishes. Nail this rebellous will of mine to thy cross, so that it may never more be able to detach itself from thee and thy holy will. I shall do it myself, O Lord, in order to please thee. I offer myself and consecrate myself entirely to thy good pleasure, my Lord and my God.

POINT II.—The almost lifeless Jesus being fastened to the cross, his tormentors raise him in the air, in the sight of heaven and earth, which are horrified at such a spectacle. Draw near, my soul, to the foot of the cross, and meditate upon the pains, enumerate the wounds, and try to feel for the untold sufferings of thy crucified Lord. There is thy Jesus, all livid and streaming with blood, hanging by three nails, naked, covered only with confusion and wounds, between two thieves, offering his great sacrifice for the salvation of sinners. Gaze upon him awhile, and shed at the sight one tear of sorrow and grief; at least weep for thy sins that have brought him to such a state. He hangs from the cross in a sea of sorrows, and there is not one to offer him the least comfort, nay, all concur in tormenting in every way anew. His head, crowned with thorns, can rest nowhere without new pain. His shoulders are flayed and torn, his bones dislocated, his hands and feet pierced through, all his members swollen and covered with blood, and his blood continues to flow still from so many sources, pleading for us with the divine justice. My soul, this is the blood which has so often cleansed thee from thy sins, and sanctified thee in the sacraments. This is the blood shed with such love and suffering by the Son of God, in order to redeem thee from sin and hell, but so often trampled by thy sins. Adore this divine blood, and kiss in spirit the sacred wounds from which it flows; gather it into thy heart, and make it a precious bath for thy uncleanness. Embrace with affection this blessed wood on which thy Saviour is suspended; press thyself close to this tree of life, in order to gather therefrom the sweet fruits of the blood and death of the Son of God. Never forget the excess of his charity, and whenever thou seest a crucifix, say: *Behold, how far the love of a God has gone for me.*

My crucified Redeemer, I adore thee, I love thee, I thank thee. I kiss reverently those hands and feet, nailed for me to the painful tree of the cross. I detest, with all my heart, my many offences against thy infinite goodness; and I beseech thee to blot them out with this precious blood, which flows so copiously from thy wounds for my salvation. Pour it, dear Jesus, upon my soul, that it may be purified and sanctified by it, and may become, through thy merits, rich in virtue and heavenly gifts. Bless me, O loving Saviour, with those hands, which are pierced for my love, and let thy blessing be an earnest of my eternal salvation. So fill my heart with thy divine love, that every love which is not for thee may be completely extinguished in me; and that I may have no other wish but that of pleasing thee. O infinite good, my crucified love, thee alone do I wish to love; thee alone do I wish to please in my every thought, in my every action.

Point III.—Return again to look upon thy Jesus nailed to the cross, and realize, by thy faith, who this Man of Sorrows is, who hangs from this disgraceful gibbet in such a painful manner. This crucified One, whom thou observest, my soul, buried in an ocean of sufferings, of reproaches, and shame, is none else than that God—immense and infinite, that sovereign and omnipotent Lord, upon whose will everything created depends. He is the only-begotten Son of God, the most mighty King, of incomprehensible majesty and grandeur, descended from the throne of his glory, in order to ascend this throne of suffering, and thereby sacrifice himself on the bloody altar of the cross for thy salvation. This crucified

One, derided, insulted, and blasphemed by all, is none other than the Saviour of men, promised from the beginning of the world, desired and prayed for with so many longing sighs, come at length to bring salvation to his people, and by this very people voted to this death. He is the most just, the most holy, the most amiable of all men, and loves man most intensely, and yet by men so cruelly treated. This crucified One suffers the most bitter pains without relief, without comfort. He suffers in all the members of his most sacred body, in all his corporal senses, even his very soul is supremely desolate. His eyes are pained by the sight of enemies, insulting and mocking him; his ears, by their atrocious blasphemies; his mouth, by a burning thirst, which they attempt to assuage only by a draught of bitter gall. His intellect is pained by the knowledge of the sins of men, and of their ingratitude; his heart, by sadness, by irksomeness, and deathlike woes. He suffers the shame of nakedness before an immense multitude of people; he suffers in his honour, by being crucified between two thieves, as their chief, on a mount allotted to the punishment of malefactors At least, the eternal Father will give some relief to his beloved dying Son. But no; he is inexorable, even to the denying him the smallest consolation that might sweeten the bitterness of his torments. Oh, how sorrowful and pitiful is the state of Jesus on the cross! See what you have done by sinning: you have crucified him, and crucified him thus. This thought alone, my soul, ought to be enough to burst thy heart for very grief and love towards the goodness of thy Jesus, so cruelly treated by thee. Ah! compassionate, at least, the loving Redeemer; thank him for his great charity; kiss anew these wounds, these fountains of salvation; bathe thyself in the precious blood which flows from the cross; offer to suffer thyself for the love of him who has so much loved thee.

Ah! my Jesus, wherefore art thou nailed to the cross, except it be to reconcile me, by the sacrifice of thy life, and the shedding of thy blood, to thy divine Father; except it be to satisfy, by thy painful death, for the debts contracted with the divine justice by my accursed sins? Now, I know, O Lord, what a great evil is one only mortal sin, if its cancelling needed the blood and death of a God-man upon the cross. I thank thee, dear Jesus, for that incomparable love thou didst bear me, which made thee willingly die, because thou hadst not the heart to see me die eternally. Oh, the excess of thy charity, which wished for nothing ever so ardently as my salvation; and for its sake, this cross, whereon thou art stretched, torn, bleeding, dying! Ah! dear Saviour, do fulfil that promise of thine, of drawing everything to thyself, when once thou wouldst be elevated on this cross. Draw this heart of mine to thee; draw it away from vice; draw it off from created things; nay, tear it out of my very breast, in order that it may be united to thee for ever by love and imitation. Make this my heart to be for ever thine entirely, and that it may never love nor do a thing displeasing to thy sovereign goodness.

Pious Practice and Fruit.

Adore to-day the five wounds of Jesus Christ, and, in their honour, perform five acts of mortification. Keep, all this day, in spirit, close to the cross of Jesus, and frequently offer his blood and passion to the eternal Father, for the pardon of your own sins and the conversion of sinners. If you love your cross, love also your crucifiers, by loving those who vex, who contradict and calumniate you, after the example of your crucified Jesus.

SATURDAY.

CONSIDERATION.—*Jesus' Agony and Death.*

POINT I.—Three hours did our loving Redeemer hang nailed to the cross to satisfy the divine justice for the sins of men; and for the time he did nothing but writhe and suffer in fearful agony, without the least assuagement. Before Jesus dies, come near, my soul, reverently to his cross, to meditate on and compassionate his last pains. Look at his tearful eyes, his pallid features, livid pierced limbs, his whole body with life ebbing out of it by slow degrees of pain. Observe his loving heart, how its palpitation grows weaker, how the divine blood no longer flows, but issues drop by drop. Observe how his adorable head, being no longer able to keep up for weakness and pain, slowly and sweetly droops, as if to give the last kiss of peace and reconciliation to men, and thereby assure them of his love. Consider how his soul, merged in a sea of bitter sadness, is about leaving his exhausted bleeding body. What does thy heart do at such a sight? Does it not feel itself moved by love and compassion for thy dear Spouse—thy loving Brother, who is dying for love of thee? Wilt thou be harder than the rocks, whioh, at the death of their Creator, burst asunder for pity, as it were? Look again, for the last time, O my soul, upon thy Redeemer alive, upon his bed of torment, upon his throne of ignominy, and reflect that this God of infinite majesty is dying for thee, monster of ingratitude, so guilty, so wicked. Yes, a God dies for thee—dies for love of thee. Arouse thyself, and come with confidence and love to the throne of his goodness, and find out, in thy dying Saviour, what thy sins have done. Consider what thou hast cost Jesus, what thou owest him; thou hast cost the life of a God. Thou owest thy whole self to a God who hast so loved thee as to lay down his life for thee. Ah! consecrate thyself speedily to the service and love of thy dying Lord. Tell him, and declare to him, that thou never again wilt offend so loving a Father, so good a God.

O Saviour of men, to what extremes has thy love brought thee! Oh, excess of the divine mercy! Oh, infinite greatness of the love of God! And what shall I do, O Saviour, to correspond with so much, such excessive love! I thank thee with my whole soul for having willed to die for me, and save me from the eternal pains of hell. I thank thy loving heart for having loved me so tenderly, and having shed so much blood to blot out my sins, and merit heaven for me. I am sorry for having loved thee so little, my Saviour, up to this, for having corresponded so little, nay, returned injuries to thy goodness. I wish and will to love thee with my whole heart. I wish and resolve never more to forget thee crucified for me.

POINT II.—Consider the thoughts and affections of the heart of Jesus, now about to die. This great High

Priest remained upon the altar of the cross, offering, with infinite love, the great sacrifice of himself for the salvation, of men. His mind, his heart, was entirely occupied in beseeching his Father, with sighs and groans, to pardon sinners, and you amongst them. He besought him, with most feeling tenderness, not to regard the demerits, the ingratitude of men, but his own sufferings, his wounds, and the sacrifice of his life. At the same time he loved men so much, as to declare that he died joyfully, and was ready to suffer more, and shed more blood, if possible, for their sakes. He pressed all men to his bosom, with the burning desire of making all partakers of his death and passion. He tenderly compassionated their miseries, and prepared a bath of his own divine blood for the wounds of their souls. To men he left, as an inheritance, the infinite treasure of his merits, of his labours, his sufferings, and his death, that they might therewith be enriched with heavenly gifts, and purchase to themselves the glory of paradise.   One thing alone remained to Jesus dying, and that was his beloved mother, Mary; her, too, he left in legacy as a loving mother to all men.   Oh! love of Jesus for men.   What more could Jesus have done for you?   What more could he have given you, after he had given you himself, and shed the last drop of blood from his veins for you?   Oh, how much are you under obligation to this divine Redeemer!   On account of him, and of his death, you have been made an adopted child of God, destined to the inheritance of heaven, and have had your sins pardoned so many times. Through Jesus you have enjoyed so many good things, so many graces, and would have gotten many more if you had not ungratefully refused to accept them, and despised them. Through Jesus you hope to have a share in the endless happiness of the saints. Through Jesus you are not now in hell, where you deserved to be so often.   See now if Jesus, dying on the cross, does not love you specially, pray particularly for you, and entreat his Father for singular favours for yourself? And you, how do you love Jesus? How have you at heart the giving him pleasure, by a virtuous and Christian life, by works of piety and mercy, by the faithful practice of his teaching? A friend who loves you, and bestows a gift on you now and again, can bind your heart to his, and fill you with love for him; and Jesus, who has loved you so much, bestowed so many priceless blessings on you, who is dying on a cross for you, cannot gain a little of your love! Ah! before he expires, beg of him to place your heart in his, and inflame it with love in this burning furnace of charity. Beseech him to detach it from all earthly affection, so that it may be wholly consecrated to the love of Jesus—Jesus crucified.

I would offer thee something, my most amiable agonizing Redeemer, in return for so much love, for so many blessings; but I have nothing but a soul covered with the leprosy of sin, and a cold carnal heart. This is the soul which thou hast loved even unto death, and for which thou hast shed thy blood. This soul I offer thee, that thou mayest purify it, sanctify it, and make it worthy of thee. I offer thee my heart, that thou mayest cleanse it from its guilty passions, from its wrong affections, and inflame it entirely with thy love. Bind me, press me to thyself, so that I may never more be separated from thee. The world, creatures, earth shall rob me no more of my heart; thou alone wilt for ever be the God of my heart; thee alone shall I love henceforth. Take away from my heart every chord of affection that might possibly hinder me in loving thee, and cause, by thy powerful grace, that all my love may be to thee, my crucified lover.

POINT III.—Now that the last moment of his mortal existence is drawing nigh, Jesus collects the last efforts of his weak and expiring powers, and, in a dying voice, commends his soul into the hands of his eternal Father. He offers himself once more as a victim to the divine justice for the salvation of men; he bows his languid head in token of the profound submission with which he accepts of death; he shuts his divine eyes, and, between the arms of the cross, gives up the ghost. Jesus is dead! After so many and such cruel tortures, being satiated with reproach and ignominy, and drowned in an ocean of suffering—Jesus dies! The loving Jesus, consumed no less by the atrocity of his pains than by the fire of his love, dies! Oh! which of us who has to live can wish to live for aught than solely to love our Jesus? Which of us, who has to suffer, would not wish to suffer for the love of Jesus? Who will refuse to stand at the foot of the cross, to contemplate and love his beloved crucified, to lament the sins that made him die, and die of grief for Jesus, and with Jesus? Jesus dies for our sins: who will be so cruel, so inhuman, as to repeat this death by sinning again? This most loving shepherd dies to give his life for his dear sheep: who will be so ungrateful as to take no share in his sorrows, in his death? Who at the sight of a God dead for love and sorrow, can give himself up a prey to the foolish pleasures of the world, to vanities, frivolities, and sin? Ah! my Jesus, Calvary will be for the future my sojourn; thy death shall be the continual subject of my reflections, my feelings, and my tears. At the death of Jesus, the sky is darkened, the sun is eclipsed, the earth quakes, the mountains split open, the veil of the temple is rent, all nature seems to rave with desolation at the sight of a God dying. And thou, my soul, wilt thou be insensible to so sad and fearful a spectacle? Will not thy heart also heave and burst with tenderness and sorrow? Look upon the lifeless and torn body of thy dead Saviour, and know for once what an evil sin is, since it has done this deed. What a blessing paradise is, which has cost such a price! What is thy own worth and value, since so much has been given for thy redemption? Oh! what a crying injustice wilt thou be guilty of if thou continuest to love the devil, the world, and sin, instead of this God, dead upon the cross for thee? Oh! how monstrous must be thy hardness of heart, if thou be not moved to compassion and tears at such a sight! Come to thy senses, my soul; the devil has not died for thee, the world has not shed one drop of blood for thee: therefore, not to them, but to him who did this for thee, dost thou belong. Jesus thou oughtest to love, for Jesus thou oughtest to live, Jesus's thou oughtest to be. Resolve this moment.

O Jesus, crucified and dead for the love of me, thou alone art infinitely amiable and worthy of all love. I do not intend to love the world any more; I do not wish to love creatures; I wish to love only thee, who hast loved me so excessively. Thee I choose for the sole and eternal object of my whole love. I wish to think always of thee, of thee suffering and dying for my sake. To thee shall I raise up my sight, to thee shall I breathe my affections, to thee shall I direct my desires, nor shall this heart of mine ever long but for thee, to whom I now offer and consecrate it. I am resolved never more, dear Jesus, to offend thee, never more to displease thee. Oh! how it grieves me to have lived so long, forgetful of thee, a stranger to thee, an enemy of thee, who hast loved me with a love so boundless! I do not deserve to live any longer; but if thy goodness deigns to prolong my life, it shall all be employed in loving thee, in meditating on thy sufferings, in bewailing my sins. Here, O Jesus, is my soul; since it has been dearly purchased by thee, make it be thine for ever, and do not let me ever again abandon it to the devil and to sin, which I hate and detest above all evils, and never shall commit at the peril of my life.

Pious Practice and Fruit.

This day look often on your crucifix, kiss lovingly and reverently the sacred wounds, and press it to your heart.

Consecrate yourself to-day to meditate in a more particular manner on the death Jesus endured for your sake. Abstain from some useless diversion, and sacrifice it to Jesus. When going to rest, think in what state you would wish to be found at the hour of death, and if you be not in that state now, try to regain, as soon as possible, the grace and friendship of Almighty God, and ask of Jesus, through the merits of his painful death, to give you the grace of a holy death.

PRAYER to which Pope Pius VII. hath annexed a Plenary Indulgence, which all the Faithful may obtain, who, after having confessed their sins with contrition, and received the Holy Communion, shall devoutly recite it before an image or representation of Christ crucified.

BEHOLD, O good and most sweet Jesus, I cast myself upon my knees in thy sight, and with the most fervent desire of my soul I pray and beseech thee that thou wouldst impress upon my heart lively sentiments of faith, hope, and charity, with true repentance for my sins, and a firm desire of amendment, whilst with deep affection and grief of soul I ponder within myself, and mentally contemplate thy five most precious wounds; having before my eyes that which David spake in prophecy: "They pierced my hands and my feet; they have numbered all my bones."

CONTENTS.

SUNDAY.

MONDAY.

THE END.